D1707236

THE
FALSE MAGIC KINGDOM
CYCLE

Jordan Krall

DYNATOX MINISTRIES

East Brunswick – Borneo – Fisherville

Published by
DYNATOX MINISTRIES

http://dynatoxministries.com

The stories in this book
have been previously published separately by
COPELAND VALLEY PRESS
in 2012.

ISBN-13: 978-1496087027
ISBN-10: 149608702X

CONTENTS

Introduction

Let's cut the crap and go directly to what matters: the book you are holding in your hands is simply amazing. Period. When Jordan Krall asked me to write a foreword for his trilogy, I told him I never did write intros, but I would make an exception for him because False Magic Kingdom, Bad Alchemy and Gog and Magog are probably among the best novellas I have read in the past ten years.

I will not tell you what the stories are about, I will not analyze their plot, will not even try to define their style – too many have tried on the few reviews I have read, and Jordan Krall's style, stories and plots are his own. Entirely, beautifully his own.

But the city described in the pages is ours. Definitely ours, as you will discover. We are there, without a doubt. And it is both scary and exciting, making you feel like the masochistic prisoner looking forward to his or her execution. We are both victims and voyeurs, caught in a web of illusions and concrete walls. All dialogues ring true, yet could be pronounced by robots.

These books have moved me deeply. And are still moving me, long after I have finished them. The humor is merciless, the irony as soft as the skin of a poisonous frog and the subliminal message as strong as a forgotten prayer.

You may think this is a strange intro for a collection – I will say "Yes, it is."

And leave you at that, letting you discover for yourself the twisted melancholic and frightening beauty of these unforgettable pages.

-Seb Doubinsky

FALSE MAGIC KINGDOM

Given that external reality is a fiction, the writer's role is almost superfluous. He does not need to invent the fiction because it is already there.
-J.G. Ballard

Dedicated
to
Teaneck Barry
& Fathers

Maybe I'm wrong, but I'll keep on saying that we're all in danger
– Pier Paolo Pasolini

A.M.

At the core of the city, the fungal magnificence of the building enthralls all who circle it. Automobiles and buses slow to let their occupants gasp or faint in ultraconscious worship of the monolithic tomb of the metropolis. Meditative pedestrians stalk the black mossy glass while idly sipping their coffee and cursing the banality of their lives. Their knees weaken; they fight the urge to fall to the sidewalk in supplication for to acquiesce so easily is a terrible transgression. They stare into the glass and attempt to see into the foyer. They yearn to see the workers. It is an important time.

It is the beginning of the work day.

*

Inside the basement, three men begin work on copying several texts. Though the cement room makes for an unconventional scriptorium, it is the only place the men could expect to complete their work without fear of interruption or infiltration. It is a psychic safe house, a bastion of textual security.

The trio use ink, paper, and computers to complete their task. They are not ignorant of the advantages of civilization's advancement in the realm of technology but they prefer the old methods as well. It is a matter of doing all within their power to preserve the words: every syllable, every concept in all forms and incarnations. Every aspect of the texts has to be kept perfectly in sync with the originals. If not, the basement triad will find themselves feasting on the cement that surrounds them. The business they are involved in is serious. It is an important time.

It is the beginning of their work day.

America is not so much a nightmare as a non-dream.
-William S. Burroughs

I. ARGON SEIZURE

Someone once told me the hotel was primed for demolition. Like always, I had responded with skepticism.

I have never seen anything get destroyed. I have never seen anything ruined or in any state of decay. Perhaps I have lived a sheltered life but for all I know, every object, person, and idea is immune to any form of degeneration or decay. People, objects, and thoughts are frozen in time but allowed to move just enough to give the impression of progress, of an eventual movement towards some destiny far off in the future. It will be a future of sameness and of an unchanged maturity.

But, like I said, perhaps I have lived a sheltered life.

When I arrive at the hotel, I find out that my room is on the top floor for which I am pleased. Despite not liking water in general, I am looking forward to a good view of the ocean. It is better than looking out at the city with all its buildings puffing smoke, noise, and artificial light. There are too many people in the city, too many busy people who live to work and work to live. The ocean provides a blank slate for my thoughts whereas the urban landscape provides nothing but a reminder of the unnatural state of things, at the chaos that eats away at the very soul of a human being. Of course, it is not something I have ever witnessed personally but I have heard stories about cities and I wish to see no decay.....only stillness and some form of purity. I do not even want to catch a whiff of urban putrefaction. So this is why I was glad to have the view of the water.

Upon entering the hotel room, I see that the housekeeper must have spent a good amount of time getting it ready. Everything is immaculate, even the television remote control which, from what I have heard, should be the filthiest thing in the room.

I sit on the bed, exhausted from the trip but not exhausted enough to lie down and nap. Sleep would be needed eventually but not yet. Things have to be done before I can give myself the luxury of dreaming.

The windows appear freshly washed. It is as if there is no glass separating me from the outside. I stand up and walk over to check for sure that there is something preventing me from falling out of the building. I put my hand out and touch the warm smoothness of the glass. I am worried its temperature will soon rise to the point of melting. I do not want to be burned by fiery glass. I do not want to fall out of the window.

I pull my hand away for it is like touching a warm corpse.

Still, I stay put, looking out and watching the dark green sea as it ripples and pulsates. After staring into its surface for a few minutes, I go back to the bed and turn the television on with the freshly cleaned remote control.

Television provides me with life outside of my thoughts. But maybe I just like the noise. It produces sounds I don't have to take part in, voices I don't have to respond to. It is a way of being a part of society *without actually taking part in society.*

Therefore I have little need of real friends or family. Instead, I let the television programs act as the outside chaos that would otherwise engulf my senses and emotional stability. Television broadcasts never decay. They are, in a way, *eternal.*

I never followed any particular program, though. I do not make any effort to have the television on at any particular time. I let my whim dictate my interactions with the shows. The randomness of my viewing exposes me to a myriad number of life experiences. I never know what the day will bring.

This particular hotel room television is ancient. I am sure one of the dust-covered speakers is blown out because the noise sounds lopsided and muffled which makes everything that comes out of it resemble slow ocean waves. I am soothed into a state of calm.

It is during this state of calm that the hotel starts to collapse.

One would think such an event would be frightening and disorienting but I find it a relief, something akin to an orgasm. There is a rumbling below me and I feel the bed drop out from under me and I am falling, the ceiling following me down along with the television. It is a dreamlike freefall. It cocoons my body in dust and noise. Every solid object turns to brown mist and I am engulfed in a noisy removal from the spider web of my existence.

I should have known this would happen. Someone once told me the hotel was primed for demolition. But like always, I had responded with skepticism.

II. SMOKE METAL FIRMAMENT

Grey plumes and ash with skin cells and copier paper, coffee cups, paperclips, staplers and Scotch tape, liquid paper fireworks, fluttering manila folders as death-birds.

Dr. Sotos is standing on the sidewalk, smoking a cigarette. He knows it is silly to do so but he's never one to be above doing silly things. Life is silly, he thinks. Life and all that it brings.

He is immune to the screaming and the blossoming emotions surrounding him. He is immune to the possibility that there is something other than research to be done in the immediate aftermath of the experiment. All experiments are a gift. All experiments must be treated as such.

Dr. Sotos appreciates this gift. He finds joy in it. One can still find joy in serious research.

The people who surround him are preoccupied with the manifestations of the experiment. They marvel and fear the overt machinations of the grand laboratory. Dr. Sotos pities the fact that they may never know the inner workings of his science.

More plumes, more debris and flapping wings of death-birds. More people decide to be "happy-go-lucky" and take to the skies or rather this is what Dr. Sotos imagines. The "happy-go-lucky" ones get a lucky transition, a lucky shot.

Their last shot at heaven.

Dr. Sotos flicks his cigarette into a pile of ashes and runs down the street, screaming nonsense words and babbling. No one appears to notice. They are still preoccupied with the manifestations of the experiment. This makes Dr. Sotos happy. He runs faster now, wondering when he'll get his last shot.

III. A VILE VEIL

My coffee cup slides across the desk and my paperclips fall to the floor. Someone looks out the window and shouts.

I think to myself, "Shut the hell up, you lousy bastards." But now someone else is shouting. Everyone in the office is on their feet, looking at the window, looking at what? A solar eclipse? I am pretty sure you aren't supposed to look directly into a solar eclipse so I think my coworkers are just a bunch of idiots. Then again, I've always thought that.

I look at my computer and feel at ease when I see the new picture I've downloaded.

But I can't resist looking back at my idiot coworkers. What the hell are they doing? Now their faces are touching the window glass and they're just staring silently. Well, at least they're being quiet now.

I stand up slowly to see what the hell they're looking at but I see nothing. They're just looking at blue sky and only blue sky.

I sit back down.

I look at the new picture and decide to print it out. I'll leave copies of it around the office. It might get some people upset but I think it might be worth it. The picture is significant to me and therefore I think I should be allowed to share it. Freedom of expression is important.

No one notices I am printing out fifty copies of the picture. Usually they frown over the waste of resources but right now everyone is swaying as if they're singing a hymn. It's like they're thinking God holds them in his hands and all that. He cradles all of us, has the whole world in his grip and he won't let us go.

All I know is, whatever they're doing, I'm not participating in it. I'm not taking part in some bizarre team building exercise. It's probably some pointless lesson in eliminating negativity or something. Not necessary. I'm not a team player. Never have been, never will be. I only work because I need money. Isn't that the only reason why people work? If we were all given the chance to sit home and watch television while having all our needs taken care of, wouldn't we jump at the chance? Hell yeah, we would. Most people don't work for the love of the job. Perhaps they learn to in order to save them from some devastating epiphany that will lead to suicide but most of us just work for the paycheck.

I expect my co-workers to start singing some company hymn but no song is coming out of their mouths. They are just babbling and shouting.

Fine. They've suckered me into it.

I walk over to the window to see what the fuss is about.

IV. BLACK BONED BUILDING

When one calls the Henwich offices, a recorded voice answers with the following:

"Thank you for calling Henwich, formally Henwich & Bingen. We value your call. If you know your party's extension, please press it now. Otherwise stay on the line to speak to an operator......"

If one does not press an extension or zero, a recorded voice says the following:

"If you know your party's extension, please. If you know your party's extension, please. If you know your party's extension, please. Otherwise stay on the line to speak to a <static/white noise> bla...giraf..."

If one still does not press an extension or zero, the recorded voice continues:

"<static/whitenoise>...bla...giraf...bla...giraf... To speak to Minoru Yamasaki dial one thousand three hundred forty seven. For Chizuo Matsumoto dial one thousand three hundred forty one...or, please hang up and try <white noise>"

At this point, most people would choose one of the options or hang up. However, if one was to choose to stay on the line, this is what will be heard:

"Gin gin gin gin gin gin gin gin gin gin gin gin gin gin.." (ad nauseum)

V. AND THE THRONE REMAINS UNMOVED

Eating a bagel. Drinking ginger ale. Reading a book.

That is what I am doing. Now I am interrupted by the stewardess who asks if I need anything else. I shake my head. I do not need anything else.

To my left, a man and his wife ask her for water. They are loud. I do not know why. It is too early in the morning to use such loud voices. That is why I've brought my book: to avoid having to talk to people.

Conversations kill my mornings.

Mornings are for meditation, for the gathering of knowledge, for spirituality, for peacefulness. Why don't these people understand? Are they incapable of appreciating the absence of unnecessary sound?

For most of my life, morning has been a time of silence. When I was a child, my parents would not utter a word before noon and made me do the same. It was simply something I was used to doing. However, I soon rebelled and would whisper words into my pillow as the rising sun crept through the window of my room.

First the dialogue consisted of nonsense words. I did not dare say real things into the pillow. Maybe I thought real words would be too blasphemous and slaughter the silence and of course, being a kindhearted child, I wanted no slaughter.

Eventually I started using real words and was relieved to find there was no apparent slaughter (a secret slaughter, perhaps, maybe one that would come to haunt me decades later. There could be some latent slaughter I hadn't noticed nor haven't to this day. There are, no doubt, deep psychological factors at play.) I made conversation about many things. At one point I had a discussion with my pillow about the strategies and

20

tactics of troops in an imaginary war of my own creation. My pillow responded with similarities between this imaginary war and the Battle of Mons Graupius. I was stunned at the comparisons and became quite adept at analyzing the mistakes of the imaginary soldiers in order to approve their chances in future battles.

Eventually my parents caught wind of my ritual and they quickly put an end to it. They were appalled at my pillow talk. They had me do chores (in silence) until noon at which time we would begin to chat incessantly.

Despite their doctrine of silence I loved my parents dearly. I realized what they had wanted was for me to gain an acute appreciation of silence. They succeeded. That appreciation I have carried with me into adulthood. The old saying is quite accurate: silence is golden. But some people simply do not understand this fact.

The man and his wife drink their water loudly, slurping and gulping grotesquely. I am tempted to tell them to be quiet, to say, "Shhhhhh!" and watch them look at me in social shock. After all, how dare some stranger tell them to be quiet? They would be mortified. They would be angry. They would be convinced I was an unstable curmudgeon.

But that would require me to add more noise to the already frustrating din.

If I was to create that disturbance, however, if I was going to correct them and cause a socially awkward situation, who would really be at fault? The reason for my silence is not just to benefit my peace of mind. It is also for them as well. It is consideration of my surroundings and their own well-being.

Would they care about that? No. They have been bred to babble. They have been raised on chatter. If they had known the basics of construction, they would have erected a new Tower of Babel in reverence to their insignificant words. They would have toiled in the sun and in the moonlight to build an obnoxious ziggurat for their worship of voices. Their chatting would bring the blue sky crashing down. All plant and animal life would cease to exist. But I'd like to think if there is a God, the deity would no doubt crush them with a silent plague.

But the man and his wife next to me do not look as if they could build such a tower. Their ambitions are much more insignificant if they have any at all. They lack the intellectual endurance for such an endeavor.

The roar of the plane is loud enough and I do not feel the need to contribute to that noise especially this early. This beautiful September morning is being ruined by all of the purposeless chatter.

But I remind myself that I should have sympathy. The man and his wife may have had parents who simply let them talk and talk and talk without any limit as to how much hot air they could pump out of their mouths. I pity them. I extend a mental gesture of empathy.

I drink my ginger ale. I try to read my book, try to ignore their slurping and gulping and talking and talking and talking. At one point they try to spark a conversation with me but I point to my neck to convey that I have a sore throat (though I do not) and they shake their heads with sympathetic understanding. They tell me to ask the stewardess for some hot tea. It will help my throat, they say. I nod and take a drink of my ginger ale. It tickles my throat and wonder: did I just jinx myself? Will I get a sore throat because of my lie? I do not usually subscribe to that sort of superstitious nonsense but my unbelief does not negate the reality of it if, indeed, it is a true reality.

Just like my unbelief in God (or a god) does not negate the reality, the possibility, that there is a higher power in charge of the universe. However, I do believe if there is a God, it is one that does not necessarily care about me or my fellow humans.

If there is a God, he (she?) is most likely deranged and sadistic. I imagine a drooling hunchback who spends its eternal days masturbating and drawing blood with its mangled teeth. This God watches us, destroys us, sends its malevolent thoughts into the world for its amusement and our punishment. This God's thoughts consist mainly of rape and murder. This mentally-retarded hunchback of the heavens gets particular pleasure out of seeing young children abused and exploited. Then this hunchback's heavenly drool falls from the sky in the form of hurricanes and dandruff in the form of disease. This is the deity I imagine when people talk of God.

The man and his wife lose interest in me and start to talk to each other about some political-religious topic of the day and I am forced to listen. I listen to their babbling. I listen to their simplistic conclusions and I wonder, "Are these people real people? Or perhaps they are just automatons put in place simply to annoy me." This thought is not necessarily a paranoid one. Scientists are doing research on artificial intelligence and the couple does look a bit artificial. The woman's face is too tan as if her creator overcompensated with the make-up. The man's face is too sharp. The bone structure does not look natural. He, too, appears to be wearing make-up.

Because of this possibility, I do not even entertain the idea of joining in their conversation to prove them wrong, to bring their ignorance to the forefront of their consciousnesses. I am a gentleman, really. I do not like to speak to people in such a condescending manner. Instead, I just keep the thoughts to myself because, after all is said and done, that's all we have: thoughts. Thoughts are our own and as much as we want to think we control the thoughts, we cannot. They are transmissions from around us filtered through our past thoughts and updated in a babbling brook of information. I see people as a culmination of their thoughts which end up coming to fruition in the form of their actions.

You must understand that I am not conceited. I am not too smart for my own good. I am not a know-it-all. I am simply a man who is leaving his home and business in Boston to make a new life for himself in Los Angeles.

Hopefully this new life will consist of a carefully structured life of silence. I am joining a commune that is based on a philosophy similar to my own. Half the day is spent in silence. The other half is spent in philosophical discussions and reading of silence-based texts. I cannot imagine a better life. And it only cost me ten thousand dollars for the first year after which I will have to find employment in order to pay for my room and board. It is all perfectly reasonable.

I sit and try to block out the talking next to me. If I was prone to anger, I would tell them to shut up but I am not that type of person. I am quite tolerant. I let the automatons talk and talk and talk and talk and talk themselves into oblivion. At least I will not have to listen to them after the plane ride. I have the rest of my life to look forward to, all that silence, all that wisdom and knowledge I shall gain from likeminded people.

In my peripheral vision, I notice the stewardesses performing some sort of grotesque play. She is being stabbed by a young, dark man. I do not know what is happening. I do not want to listen to their screams. I want silence.

The man and his wife cower in their seats. The wife is crying hysterically while her husband closes his eyes and mutters a prayer.

Things get worse and I cover my ears for fear of more sound.

This grotesque play is taking a terrible, terrible turn.

VI. THE COLLATERAL WINDS

There is something about the city that makes Jessica ill.

It might have been the car exhaust or the pollution in general but then she thinks it is the sheer majesty of everything. The buildings do indeed seem to scrape the sky, they are frightening and godlike. They are unnatural.

Jessica hails a cab and tells the driver to go back to her hotel. The driver does not speak English and the address needs to be repeated several times before he understands. He nods and speeds down the street. Jessica leans forward in case it is necessary to give more directions.

The cab arrives at the hotel without incident. Jessica is a little bit disappointed. There was a part of her that wished for some unique event to happen during her drive.

It would have been like a film and she would find herself in the midst of drama. Life can be so disappointing sometimes. Is it too much to ask for a car chase or an explosion?

She pays the driver and stands in front of her hotel, looking up at it and wondering if anyone had ever tried jumping from it. She knew it was a morbid thought but it was the sort of thing she found difficult to avoid. After all, her father had committed suicide by jumping out of a hotel window. Jessica had only been nine years old and from what she could remember, nothing prior to the suicide would have given her any clue as to why he would have done it.

One of Jessica's friends in college had suggested her father was a victim of government mind control considering he had done some computer work for them.

Jessica didn't buy into that theory but that same college friend had given her a dozen books about experiments the government had conducted on their own citizens. Interesting, yes, but Jessica knew it was all just junk to satisfy the subculture of paranoia. Her father had not been a victim of LSD experiments or electrode abuse. The man was disturbed and had decided to jump to his death. That was all.

That was all there was to it: just a hotel suicide by a computer programmer who had happened to work for the government for a short period prior to his death. He had most likely suffered from some mental illness and had done a good job of hiding it from his family.

Jessica walks into the hotel lobby and navigates around the tourists and businessmen. One man in particular looks her up and down. No doubt he imagines her spread-eagled on the bed in his hotel room. She would be drunk or drugged, drooling and semi-conscious. It wouldn't be rape, not in his eyes. It would just be a power play, a pressured persuasion. The man will justify it, tell himself that Jessica is starving for love, starving for intercourse, and that he is doing her a favor. Or, he may think, "She's a stuck up bitch and deserves everything she gets." He hasn't decided what excuse he will give himself to soothe his conscience.

Jessica quickly walks away from the man, from all men, all women, too. Women could be just as cruel, sadistic, and lustful. She heads for the elevators.

The elevators are the worst. She hates them. To be packed into a small room like that, well, that was a nightmare from which she couldn't escape. Taking the stairs wasn't an option. She was fifteen floors up and the stairway looked dim and dangerous, a haven for deviants and would-be rapists.

The elevator comes quickly and she gets on along with a half dozen others whose faces she does not pay attention to. For all she knows, they have the blank features of manikins. They could be hotel automatons whose only function is to give the appearance of a busy hotel. She doesn't know if that's a comforting thought or not. After all, wouldn't automatons be capable of rape, too? It would be worse because it would be a mechanical violation, passionless and cold.

This is an absurd idea. Jessica knows this. She thinks it might be a side effect of her medication. What is the medication supposed to do for her? She can't remember. She only knows the side effects. The daydreams are too much like real thoughts. She wonders if her father was on medication. If not, maybe he should have been. Then perhaps he would not have jumped. Or maybe, he was on medication and that is what sent him over the literal edge.

Jessica holds her breath in the elevator and waits for it to reach her floor. She gets out. She is the only one to do so on that floor and for that, she is thankful. Thankful to who? She doesn't know. She doesn't believe in God. She doesn't believe in anything really, nothing above and beyond what she can see and experience in her life. Once her father was gone, there was no reason to believe in a higher power.

As Jessica opens her hotel room door, she thinks about God and her father. In her mind, they are one and the same. Her father fell from heaven and landed on the cement like one-third of the holy trinity splattering onto the earth. Had her father been a sacrifice? Had he died for someone's sins?

Jessica sits on the bed and pulls her hair back into a ponytail. She takes out a cigarette and starts to smoke.

She lets the smoke surround her, coat her body in a coffin of smoke. She does not want to be there. She does not want to be in a hotel in Manhattan. She doesn't want to have to visit the corporate office of the company she works for.

But she has no choice.

She stares out the window. She thinks about jumping. She thinks about repeating her father's action though she knows it would be a selfish, idiotic decision. She knows it comes from a part of her brain that wants to pity itself. It is also something to do with honor, with legacy. The legacy of suicide, of giving up, of making a spectacle of oneself. Though Jessica is shy, she wants to be noticed for something spectacular.

Another part of her wants to blow the city to bits. She has no experience with bomb making but in her fantasies, in her daydreams, she is an expert in demolition. Jessica plants bombs at the root of every building in the city. No one notices because she looks so normal, so unassuming.

Then she'd find somewhere a few miles away to watch as everything explodes. She might even masturbate.

The streets below the hotel are filled with heads and machines. Jessica thinks life boils down to just that: brains and machines bustling around the city like insects. She admits to it not being an original thought; she had read about similar ideas in some of the books her friend had lent her.

She leans her forehead against the glass, looking at the insects below her. She whispers words and wishes they were bombs.

VII. SECOND BARAGOUIN

This is the morning of moldy buildings.

Puffs of inky smoke cover the ceiling-like sky, hiding the water stains and the insect trails under intangible codes of burning doctrine and asphalt. This is the last time the king will open a book.

This is the last time the king will rule.

The king's subjects lie on the sidewalk and street, their bones creaking and cracking, spilling white-noise exhaust into the air. Their groans slither through the din and split sound waves into ancient languages and stock reports.

Consonants poke candent holes through the king's doctrine. If there are vowels, they are hiding under the shroud of a guttural dogma encrypted within an interoffice memo.

With a weak but determined hand, the king pours the remains of the book into the cup and drinks. Bathic blasphemy always soothes the throat like ancient tongues enraptured by medicine. Black eggs split and sizzle in the king's stomach: a chamber of undigested commerce.

Speaking through multiple tongues, the king lifts several financial curses off his subjects, tearing their sweaty tendril-like thoughts out of the air and places them in jelly jars. Each top is screwed carefully as to not disturb the warm, obscene glass.

The king places each jar in a drawer that sits next to his throne. The throne itself has been crafted from broken and obscure texts. It was a gift from the king's father-in-law. The old man bought it in a shop in a town northwest of the kingdom. It was meant to be a frivolous curio.

It is slowly becoming a gelatinous dungeon of political theories.

The jars rattle and the throne shrieks in a morbid cacophony of exclamations and explanations. It shivers into blobs, falls to the ground, and surrounds the subjects who do not notice the creeping horror of the throne. The king mutters several words but knows the volume and tone are not sufficient to arouse his subjects from their raptus.

Crooked maps of outdated lands cover the streets in overlapping confusion of broken borders, intersections, and obsidian lakes. The king points to a spot and asks a question. The only reply is a din of arrogant disappointment.

A leather case opens and a razor is removed.

The king's face droops in masculine folds, red sparks claiming a place near his crotch. They burn holes and give birth to hungry oblivion. The aching holes contract and expand and contract and expand and squirt royal fluid across the eyes of his subjects.

Laws are made and behaviors are regulated.

Brazen gobs of drool spill out into the streets and turn into historical shapes that surround the subjects, transforming them into proud cocoons. Bags of teeth and coins are removed from hidden pockets and the teeth are strewn across the room like yellow ruins of an archaic kingship. The coins are eaten.

Small bone twigs and totems of hair recreate battles, walking across the wall maps with purposeless poise. Caves amidst the skyscrapers ejaculate insects into the theatrical fracas. Fireworks of dust and boredom are vomited into the air, blinding the king. Death-birds attack royalty.

In a matter of seconds, several things are learned. Several things are lost. Several things cease to exist.

Again: they cease to exist.

The memories slowly evaporate and are replaced with small jelly jars filled with sand and spittle. Time is simply corrected, erased and rewritten. The jars are quickly hidden in the drawer next to the throne.

The queen is sent for and she arrives in a huff.

She asks about the problem but before she can receive a reply she is bombarded by a spectrum of light and shadow, brilliance and boredom, expectations and disappointment buried in bulbous spirals of jet fuel that are being ejected from the king's cockeyed skull.

The queen reacts accordingly. She takes out her leather case and slips a razor out. It shines in the spectrum, scattering the future across the maps. Borders become scum, spreading across inches, across miles of asphalt and melted steel until the streets are a microcosmic disaster.

All the fingernails in the kingdom throw tantrums like small children, breaking away from their parents and spiting everyone, everything in their path. They join the teeth and soon the hair arrives, moving into throbbing clumps.

They ache with anticipation. They smother the queen's hand, slaughtering the razor in dark follicle movements.

The king screams.

Buildings and clouds fall and bring a deluge of jet fuel and death-bird bones.

Molecular rapture implodes. Every heart is enlarged.

Egg white seeds splatter the king's nose. Pink noise escapes small puckered speakers that have been bolted inside the sides of the throne. Primordial acoustics tremble, filling the streets with sound waves birthed of ancient spinal cords and guttural languages that have been documented into an accursed multitude of royal records and news broadcasts.

Strips of skin fall to the ground. They sizzle like bacon.

The king's subjects crawl like worms and eat the knowledge. Both king and queen act accordingly: they gather up their belongings, their razors, and leave the kingdom.

They relocate to the noisy town and shop for a new throne.

A new tomb.

Then: they cease to exist.

VIII. BUTTO BUTTO BUTTON

"This will only take a minute. I wanted to talk to you about something. Nothing major but I think it's relatively important," Ronald says.

Barry looks at his boss and forces a smile. "Sure, sure. I understand."

"It has something to do with company requirements."

"Of course. I understand."

"And those requirements, those standards, those are what keep this company afloat. It's what drives us to be the best in our field."

"Yes," Barry says. "I understand."

Ronald coughs into his fist and clears his throat. "So, there's a question I need to ask you and if you answer it honestly, I think everything will go smoothly. Please understand that you don't have to answer at all but it would be best for all of us if you did."

"Okay."

"Also understand that I'm doing this according to protocol and all company standards. I'll be taking notes on the meeting and passing it along in order to keep everything in order."

"Okay."

"You understand?"

"Yes," Barry says. "I understand."

Ronald opens a folder on his desk and looks down at it, perusing it for several minutes before he finally opens his mouth to speak. "Barry."

"Yes?"

"Okay, let's get started."

Barry nods. "Alright."

"Before I ask you the question, I'll need to confirm some basic personal information."

"Okay."

"These are questions you are required to answer."

"I understand."

Ronald looks back down at the folder. "Your full name is Barry David Bayley and your date of birth is February 23, 1983."

"That is correct."

"And you started to work for us three years ago."

"Yes, last month was my three year anniversary."

"And you originally applied for a position in R&D but eventually got interviewed for E&D. Is that correct?"

"Yes."

"Was it ever explained to you why we interviewed you for that position?"

"No, not in any great detail."

"What details were you told?"

"I was told I'd be a better fit for that department."

"What was your response to that?"

Barry shrugs. "I told them it was fine."

"During the three years you've been working in E&D, have you ever discussed with anyone your desire to change departments?"

"Discuss with who?"

"Anyone. Coworkers or otherwise."

"Well, no, I don't think I even thought about it."

"Did you ever visit the 93rd floor?"

"What do you mean?"

Ronald looks up from the folder and looks Barry in the eye. "I am asking if you have ever visited the R&D department on the 93rd floor."

"That was where I went for the initial interview and I might have been there since then, I'm not sure."

"So you cannot recall being there other than for your initial interview?"

"No, I really don't remember," Barry says. "What is this about exactly?"

"What about the 97th floor? Have you been to the 97th floor?"

"I don't remember, really. What is this about?"

"Have you ever been to the 97th floor?"

"No, I don't think so. I can't remember."

"You can't remember or you haven't been there?"

Barry sighs. "I haven't been there."

"So you're stating that you have never been to the 97th floor?"

"That is correct."

"During your time with the E&D, have you ever answered calls from the 97th floor?"

"How can I possibly remember all the calls I've answered?"

"So is that a no?"

Barry squirms in his seat. "How is this basic personal information?"

"I assure you this is the most basic set of questions and it won't take much longer if you start cooperating."

"With all due respect, how am I not cooperating?"

"Have you ever answered calls from the 97th floor?"

Barry leans back in his chair. "No, I never once answered a call from the 97th floor."

"It says here you graduated from East Ballard High School."

"Yes, I did."

"It took you an extra year to do so."

"Yes."

"Did you explain this to the person who interviewed you?"

"They never asked me about it."

"I find it hard to believe they wouldn't ask you about that."

"They didn't. They had a copy of my resume and I filled out an application for them with all the required information and they never asked about it."

"But it took you an extra year to graduate high school."

"I'm aware of that. What does it matter now?"

"Can you explain it now, please?"

"Explain what? Explain why it took me an extra year?"

Barry starts to sway back and forth in his seat. "I flunked my senior year, okay? That's it. I flunked and had to repeat the year."

Ronald nods and makes a note in the folder. He says,

"In the E&D department, there is a filing cabinet where you keep hardcopies of research. Is that correct?"

"Yes."

"And this is in addition to keeping it on the database?"

"Yes."

"Has anyone other than your coworkers in E&D have access to these files?"

"No, not that I know of," Barry says. "I imagine if someone wanted to, they could have picked the lock and gotten to the files."

Ronald leans back in his chair, coughs, and tilts his head. "What do you mean 'picked the lock'?"

"You know, I guess someone could have broken into the file cabinet if they wanted to."

"But who said anything about breaking into the cabinet? I was just asking if anyone else in any other department had access to the files."

"I'm sorry. I guess I misinterpreted the question."

"Has anyone broken into the files?"

"No, not that I know of. I just told you that."

"Barry, it seems like you are getting more and more resistant to my questions and I haven't even gotten to the matter at hand."

Barry breathes deeply. "I'm sorry. I don't mean to be resistant. I'm doing the best I can. I'll answer any question you ask."

"Thank you," Ronald says. "Now, one last basic question before we begin. When you applied to this company, you listed one reference as Henwich & Bingen. Is that correct?"

"Yes."

"It says here you worked there for six months?"

"Well, yes, it was just a paid internship program."

Ronald grunts. "How was that program?"

"It was fine."

Ronald peruses the folder for several more minutes.

"Now, let's get down to it."

"Okay."

"What the company needs to know is whether or not you are willing to move to the 97th floor as a sort of…promotion."

"You mean work for R&D?"

"No. You'd still be with E&D but you'd be working as a sort of extension of your department but on the 97th floor."

"Well, I mean, I guess. What will I be doing?"

"Pretty much the same as now except, perhaps, dealing a bit more with the people on the 97th floor."

"Okay…"

"Are you willing to apply to this promotion?"

"I have to apply?"

"Of course. You can't expect us to simply hand out a promotion."

"But you brought me in here to ask me if I wanted it."

"I was asking if you'd be interested in the promotion. Are you?"

"I said yes."

"No, you said you guess."

"Okay, I am interested," Barry says. "What do I have to do to apply?"

Ronald rolls his chair back, grabs another folder from a cabinet, and rolls back to the desk. He opens the new folder up and says, "You just have to answer a few basic questions."

IX. MANTRA U-TURN

And the theater there is made of drugged diamond planes…a person submits to and becomes a possession of…and that's that, the last showing of that Middle Eastern film. Behind the theater there is a field and children build forts and make a mess of it but that's okay because no one pays any mind. They're just kids.

They crowd around a crane (one just like in the movie they just saw) and imagine the "vampire" hanging from it. They throw rocks at the imaginary killer. After a while, they stop playing that game and move onto other things like kicking each other and running around like crazy men.

A thirteen-year-old boy (the oldest one there) finds a book buried in the field. It is small and orange. He takes the book home, brushes it off and reads it in his room, quietly as to not disturb his father.

Father. Father. Father.

The boy reads from the book…

They have decided the ones from Jupiter, from Saturn, and felt a blankness come over their bodies. In the city…they are cracks in the street and in the towns…they are cracks in the farms…jugs of fly milk scattered and bodies of cold gentlemen strung, hanging from the winds. Gholamreza! Gholamreza!

Out of the theater walks Edward Lytton who lights a cigarette and stands on the sidewalk, blowing smoke into spirals and blocks, humming and belching and singing songs within his skull to dispel the rumors he is telling himself.

He thinks he is in danger and he probably is but he tries to persuade himself to look beyond all tell-tale signs and have faith in the –

What?

Lytton does not know.

Or maybe he forgets. He doesn't know which.

He thinks about calling his one and only friend. There is a chance that might help him keep his mind off the danger. But his friend, his friend is out of the country. He is somewhere hot, extremely hot and dusty and Lytton does not envy the man. Scorpions and angry natives stinging, stinging, pulling guns and ancient books from their belts, ready to sting, sting, sting!

Edward Lytton puts his cigarette to his face, feels the heat, and tries to expand that feeling into the sunlight his friend must be feeling. He pinches himself: the sting of a scorpion to be embellished. He wants to ask his friend to keep him out of danger.

What danger, Edward? What are you talking about?

Why are you being so paranoid?

I'm not being paranoid.

Yes, yes you are. This always happens and I'm getting tired of dealing with it.

And that's that.

He puts the cigarette out on a street sign.

The thirteen-year-old boy who found the book closes it and shoves it under his bed. It is nighttime and the moon shines brightly into his room. He looks up and thinks about his friend Tommy Edgar Mitchell and wonders if he will ever find his way out of that moon crater. His mother must be worried sick.

Mother. Mother. Mother.

Gholamreza. Gholamreza. Gholamreza.

There is a delay in his speech. There is a delay in his thinking. He wonders and waits, wonders and waits. Opens his mouth to speak and waits and waits. Then the words come out, they spill out from his lips, from his tongue and teeth and shatters the air with incantations.

Overlay delay noy bus go down our lady of the grin atrocity disability star plunder noy bus go down our lady of the grin and what we can possibly think mother father mother father martyr father loss tim martyr farther muscle down our lady of the grin grinning control get into the taxi, bitch, bla gira get into the the the the the the

What? The what? No, Edward, no danger. No danger.

Just don't walk down to the Port Richmond Deli. You may not come back, Edward.

Maybe I don't want to come back.

Oh, don't say that kind of thing, Edward. Let's go to a movie. It'll get your mind off things.

I don't want to. It's always too hot in the theater.

Too hot? Come on. You know how long I was in the desert? Now that's hot.

I've never been to the desert. Is it dangerous?

Dangerous? Everywhere is dangerous, Eddie. Everywhere.

X. NOWHERE IS SAFE

Ronald walks through the door, expecting his wife to be on the couch like always, reading one of her magazines. He doesn't know why he keeps buying those things for her. They only make things worse. They reinforce her irrationality.

But she isn't on the couch.

Maybe she is making dinner. Ronald walks into the kitchen. That would be a first. The last time she had made dinner was, what, four years ago? Even then it was something she just put into the microwave.

She isn't in the kitchen.

She isn't in the bedroom either.

"Susan?" Ronald calls out. "Susan, are you home?"

No answer but he hears a noise in the basement and proceeds to walk down the stairs.

Susan is in the corner of the basement, standing in front of a shelf, stacking cans of soup and vegetables.

"What are you doing, Susan?" Ronald says.

His wife turns around. "I'm stacking cans, Ron. What does it look like I'm doing?"

"Stacking cans for what?"

Susan sighs heavily. "So we can be prepared."

"Prepared for what?"

"Why do you have to be so dense, Ron?"

"What, Susan? What am I missing? What the hell's the problem?"

"Nothing, Ron. Nothing," she says, going back to stacking cans onto the shelves.

"Just talk to me, Susan. What's wrong?"

"Everything's wrong, Ron. Everything. Have you read the paper lately?"

"Oh, not this again."

"What? What again?"

"What have you been reading?"

Susan shakes her head. "Don't you blame what I read, Ron. You always do that. You don't take me seriously. You never think I can have a thought of my own."

"That's because all your thoughts seem to come straight out of those stupid magazines."

Susan throws a can to the floor. "Shut up, Ron!"

"Okay." Ronald walks over to his wife and puts his arm around her shoulder. "I'm sorry. Okay? I'm sorry."

"Yeah?"

"Yeah. I just had a brutal day at work. Another meeting."

"With who?"

"Barry Bayley. You don't know him."

"Was it a bad meeting?"

Ronald shrugs. "Eh, wasn't good or bad. Just a meeting. A long one."

"Sorry, Ron."

"I'll get over it. So you want to tell me what's happening with this. You got enough food here to feed us for six months."

"We have to be prepared, Ron. Anything can happen nowadays. No one is safe. We have to make sure we have enough food in case we can't leave the house for a while."

"Why wouldn't we be able to leave the house?"

"Lots of reasons. Chemtrails, radiation, viruses, death squads…"

"Death squads? Seriously, Susan?"

"Yes, Ron, I'm serious."

"Where'd you read that?"

"Doesn't matter where I read it. I've read it a few places and it's true. There are death squads out there."

"Out where? The suburbs?"

"Everywhere, Ron."

"So our government is sending out death squads?"

"No. Not exactly," Susan says, putting a can down on the shelf. "It's more than that."

"Well…I'm sure we'll be just fine, Susan."

"Don't, Ron. Don't treat me like I'm a child who's afraid of monsters."

"I'm not."

"Yes, you are. Why can't you ever take me seriously?"

Ronald sighs, gives his wife a kiss on the cheek, and walks back upstairs to make himself dinner.

XI. ASTRAL BARAGOUIN PARTY

The boy stands in front of his class and reads from his notebook, "At the core of the city, the fungal magnificence of the building enthralls all who circle it…"

He receives giggles in response. His classmates do not appreciate his words nor do they understand them. But he goes on nonetheless. "Inside the basement, three men begin work on copying several texts…"

A crumpled up piece of paper hits the boy in the face.

More giggles. The teacher puts her hand up to the class and says, "Stop that right now!"

The boy ignores both the abuse and the teacher. He goes on with his reading. He turns a page of his notebook.

"One of Jessica's friends in college had suggested her father was a victim of government mind control considering her had done some computer work for them…"

The class shouts, giggles, ignores the teacher. The boy's words bring the bad behavior to a boil, causing more crumpled papers to be thrown as well as pencils and random pieces of junk the students find in their desks.

Giving up, the teacher sits down in her seat and puts her hands to her face. She listens to the boy as he goes on reading from his notebook. It was a mistake not checking the boy's work first. He was always a weird one, always having to do something odd. It probably has something to do with his father.

Oh, his father.

The teacher pities the boy even more now that she remembers his upbringing. It must be quite difficult living in that household.

A pencil flies past the teacher's face. She puts her head down and prays for sleep, inhaling the stale smell of her wooden desk as she is lulled into a trance by the boy's reading.

"Because of this possibility, I do not even entertain the idea of joining in their conversation to prove them wrong, to bring their ignorance to the forefront of their consciousnesses. I am a gentleman, really."

The students bang their fists on their desks and scream obscenities but the boy continues to read.

"…and updated in a babbling brook of information…"

XII. PEOPLE MISSING

Tina has always looked like a woman despite her having two penises.

Her parents had made the decision early on to raise her as a female because they thought it would be easier for her in the early years to identify with the gender which was most evident. When she was older, and ready to enter into a mature relationship, then they would discuss what Tina would do about divulging the truth about her body.

But Tina does not want two penises. In fact, she does even want one. To her, they are false parts, extraneous muscles unnecessary for her survival and, most importantly, her happiness. She wants freedom from phalluses altogether.

On the eve of her eighteenth birthday, she approaches her parents about the surgery she wants to have. They are adamantly against it. They tell her she should not fool with the body God had given her.

Tina responds with the question as to why God would have given her two dicks. They cringe at her use of slang.

"Why did God make me a freak?" she cries.

"God always has a plan," her mother says.

Tina retreats to her room and pulls out her bottle of Taborica. She has already taken her pill today but decides to take three more. She wants to do anything to take her mind off things.

She is now a prophet, a two-pronged desert mother/father.

God turns her anus into a vagina for she now has no need to defecate. She is a pure being and living in a cave…staring at a wall…feeling the Spirit as it passes through her cells.

She pulls out a bag of teeth and coins from the dirt floor and jingles it around. Out of the sky comes a bestial cry followed by the appearance of a large moth-like reptile that flies into the cave and around the darkness above Tina's head.

The moth-reptile starts to defecate on her….greenish liquid splattering the prophet's eyes. Tina embraces all of it and shudders into a trance. Nonsense words leak out of her mouth like vomit.

She sees thousands of slaves shaving their heads in front of their king who is holding a swordfish above his bald skull. The saints in their temples cry out and gnaw at each other's breasts.

Buildings collapse. Tiny manikins float out of the rubble. A giant marionette drops down from the sky abruptly, dances and grabs the manikins…and disappears with them into the blue blue blue morning sky…

Tina wipes feces from her eyes and starts to write in her book: an apocalypse of twin phalluses, sprouting like mushrooms from a dung pile in the cave of a new prophet. There are no serpents in the cave, no heralds of oblivious truth.

Pig demons sit at the foot of the rubble and Tina spits smoke sigils, silently silencing the swine, filling the broken offices with brilliant automatons, unblemished and binging on a babbling brook of information.

The cave fills with liquid ghosts and lynched hosts.

Tina writes a note to her parents and leaves their home for good.

I can't live like this, it says. I'm getting the operation. Bye.

Her parents weep when they read the note but they do so not out of the loss of a child, no. They weep because of God's loss of a child.

XIII. VISNA, LORD OF VACCINATIONS

Pompeii, second generation, still exists. The dust-mummies running through the streets. They exist. I can feel the heat and taste the grit but it is just my brain working overtime to communicate to me the hallucinations implanted in me. Everything I see and hear, smell, everything, is a result of the pedophile doctors and scientists who have installed memory clusters in my brain and long-term suppositories that buzz and dissolve. I see cobra heads and minarets and bearded men spinning. My eleven year old brain not knowing what or who or where, it had shut off and I had slept for 3 days.

Dr. Visna referred me to Dr. Corbelli and who referred me to Dr. Sotos. They all inspected me, evaluated me, and gave me a thorough looking over. It was disorienting and I remember a ceiling fan spinning slowly, making my eyes cross and my eyelids twitch. There was a smell like antiseptic and urine and mint candies.

"There's nothing we can do at the moment," Dr. Sotos had said, scratching his beard with his liver-spotted hand.

"But you should wait patiently like a good little girl."

He said it slowly, stretching each syllable but ending each word with a sharp tongue that violated me. We stared at each other for a few seconds and then he abruptly left the room.

The room shook and dust fell from the ceiling. Had Dr. Sotos known it was coming? Had he fled the room in fear of toxic particles? Ever since, I have felt a keen sense of hallucinatory panic.

And for weeks I received mailings from Dr. Sotos.

First, they were in the form of postcards. On one side: an obscene photograph from the 19th century. On the other: tiny print, in what I presume to be his own handwriting, detailing grotesque sexual diseases.

Next I received a box of cement rubble along with a photograph of two fingers (which I presume to be his) as well as a handful of coat buttons.

Then he called me at home. When I answered, Dr. Sotos said nothing but I knew it was him from the beard- scratching which I could hear over the phone. After a few minutes of that, he spoke.

"Are you siiiiiiiiiiiiiiiiiiiiiiiiiiiiiiiiiick?" he croaked.

I shook my head, not realizing the doctor couldn't see me. But maybe he could? Maybe he installed cameras in my house. Perhaps he pleasured himself to his video voyeurism, justifying it by telling himself it was for medical research. There are men who do such things: videotape unsuspecting women and use those videos to masturbate to as well as trade them with their fellow perverts. It is a disgusting trend.

I replied, "No, I don't…think I am."

"But you must be siiiiiiiiiiiiiiiiiiiiiiiiiiiiiiiick! You must beeeeeeeeeeeee!"

"No…"

"We have an appointment tomorrow morning. Anytime after eight will be just fiiiiiinne."

"But…okay."

"Not far….just a few…miles. One-nine-five Melrose Avenue, NW2," he said. "Got it? It is easy to miss but I don't think you will. I dooooooon't," he cooed. Then he hung up.

My twenty year old brain not knowing what or who or where, it shuts off and I sleep for an hour and then wait until eight in the morning at which time I start to walk to the address Dr. Sotos has given me.

It is now that time.

I pass vacant lots covered in rubble. I pass dust mummies as they jack off into discarded library books. They read the words while they sprout white ropes to strangle the text:

"The myth of the benandanti is connected by innumerable threads to a much larger complex of traditions which was…."

"…reports that 11,000 Roman cavalry and infantrymen…..at Mons Graupius.."

"The rainbow is a symbol representing the New Age Movement…"

"…starred in the 1934 film 'Romance in Manhattan'…"

I reach the address Dr. Sotos has given me. It is a yellow building with several apartments cut out of the structure. I locate his door and knock.

Beard-scratching…along with the sound of bare footsteps. The door opens and the doctor stands holding a model airplane.

"Welcome to Pompeeeeeeeiiiiiiiiiiiiiiiiiiiiii…."

XIV. THIRD GATEKEEPER

I will begin by saying that I do not appreciate your keeping from me the details of my father's plight. When he contracted the disease, I should have been told immediately, not so I could take any so-called proper precautions but because it would have given me ample time to prepare for the inevitable.

You are my mother. You are not the gatekeeper of knowledge. Yes, you married him but I am a part of him or rather, he is a part of me. Therefore, if any force is to destroy his body, I am to know about it. I am to be privy to any knowledge no matter how destructive it may be to my psyche. Not since childhood have you been responsible for that part of my existence.

My father's suffering, his hellish condition...I should have been aware of it all. But what is your defense? Did you think that by telling me you'd somehow pass on the suffering to me, your only son? Were you just trying to protect me? I've never been one to advocate the withholding of knowledge in any circumstance. If you had just told me, I could have handled it my own way, as an adult, as the son of a suffering man.

But now what? He just sits there, drooling, babbling.

"Blankets of spazz out krauts with drums and drugs and parachutes filled with smoke and blasts gatling fun liabilities and bonds...Bill came over looked at Texas Instruments took it apart games and BBS debates...Montville bap...bowery."

I do not wish to inherit his fate, his condition. But meditation on this fact leads me to some conclusions: leads me to autistic majesties, autistic automatons riding feathered serpents as brown station wagons that rattle.

The doctors examined me with noisy lights and diagnosed me/him with what? I cannot have all of it. If there are cures or treatments, I expect to be told about them. Did the doctors tell you? Are you withholding that information from me as well? I have every right to know. You could have picked up the phone at any time and divulged the secrets of his sickness.

Every morning I wake up and my mouth is filled with the taste of dust and jet fuel. What do I do? What do I do to stop myself from drooling and babbling? I am an adult, yes, but I am also your child. I can't stop drooling. I am suffering, too, you know.

XV. FILTHY JOKE FROM A FOREIGN LAND

Jali pours the fuel into the container and secures the top.

"To Moloch comes more kindling…" He kisses the bomb and waves to the camera. "Hello, a mere caca!"

Laughter explodes from behind the camera. Jali's friends can't help themselves. Their bellies hurt with humor and hunger. One man, however, does not laugh. It is Bunting, the cameraman, who zooms in on Jali and asks, "Is this what we are supposed to do? Just laugh like court jesters?"

"Court what?"

"Jesters! Like kings have…"

"We do not work for kings!"

Bunting shakes his head. "It is just an expression."

"Leave the expressions to the soldiers of Shaytan," Jali says. "They are the ones who worship the king in his false kingdom."

"I know that. I was just wondering if we may be letting our laughter get in the way of what we need to do. Our purpose. Our mission…"

"What we need to do is right here," Jali says, pointing to the table covered in Semtex, C4, Astrolite G, argon candles, Hi-Fi Digimonsters, Grandizer, Voltes V, OKFOL, Cordtex, adipic acid, crospovidone, PGGB lubrication, magnesium stearate, talc, and hand-rolled cigarettes.

"I think it's much bigger than that," Bunting says. "We aren't playing as children anymore, Jali."

"So what you want us to do? Not laugh when things are funny?" He looks at the other men whose eyes are looking down at the floor, not willing to get involved in the power play.

"I just didn't think it was all that funny, Jali."

"It doesn't matter what you think. You just point the camera and make sure you get me on the tape."

"There's no tape."

"What do you mean there's no tape?"

"We are using a new camera. Just uses a computer chip."

Jali throws his hands up. "It was just an expression, right? When I said get me on tape, it was just an expression!"

Everyone in the room laughs except for Bunting who zooms in on Jali's face, zooms in on the birthmark that looks like the number eleven. He imagines ejaculating on it, sending an explosion of semen against it as to destroy

Jali's cheekbones. His sperm would be like jet fuel that would burn through Jali's face and destroy the arrogance.

"Hey! Hey!" Jali says. "What's the matter with you? Why you looking at me like that, eh?"

Bunting zooms out.

XVI. THINGS FOUND IN THE RUBBLE OF THE HOTEL

Vinyl records, burnt now, melted but suitable for other things like art with superglue: *Gris-Gris* by Dr. John, *Pretzel Logic* by Steely Dan, *Hannover Interruption* by Merzbow, *Be My Twin* by Brother Beyond, *New York* by Lee Towers.

Books, twisted, tattered, brown, and crispy but good enough for collectors: *Universe Day* by K. M. O'Donnell, *A Passionate Pilgrim* by David M. Robertson, *The Grub Star Shudders* by Don Patchogue, *Ancient Evenings* by Norman Mailer, *Concrete* by Thomas Bernhard, *Thunder at Twilight* by Frederic Morton.

Odds and ends: water bottles, tin toys, plastic toys, wooden toys, papers with scribbles, pictures drawn by young children for mom/dad (no real talent evident but all the love in the world), condom wrappers, syringes, computer corpses, tubes of glue, magazines with gossip in heat, covered in sweat and jet fuel.

XVII. UNFRUITFUL WORKS OF THE BOWERY BOYS

My dad had always been a hardworking man. He did backbreaking work year after year to support his family. In his early 50s he decided to learn to play the piano which I thought was a good idea. I found it nice that he was doing something relaxing and non-work oriented, something that would keep him away from all of the other things he was preoccupied with (religious and political debates, etc).

Now, just a few years later, the prospect of playing anything on the piano is hopeless. He can barely get out of bed without assistance. He trembles. He forgets. He is delirious at times. The Parkinson's crept up slowly and then hit him fast. Here, this once strong man, six-foot-four and muscular reduced to a shriveled old specimen of regret who cannot take care of himself. He stutters and drools. I am reduced to tears.

His processing skills are getting weaker but I've always suspected he had already possessed some deficiency in that area (I have often tried telling him things about myself, my life, only to be met with silence and a blank stare) but I try to have patience when speaking to him now.

He is not the father I grew up with. He is not the strong man who was there for me, to save me, to rescue me, to be the person I look to for guidance. He is not the same man who ran down the street barefoot when a bully had slammed my head into a brick wall. I swear I saw murder in my father's eyes. The bully was lucky my father held his venomous rage inside. He would have protected or avenged me at all costs.

But the illness…

And with the illness come family secrets.

What had my father done over the years in between going to church and trying to teach me the bible? Apparently he had sinned and it was all kept secret. Now it makes some sense. Perhaps God is real and has punished my dad by striking him with this disease. But I feel guilty about thinking that way. I don't think my dad deserves this.

You should see him, how far he's come. Before he found religion, he was a bit of a hell raiser and so I understand why he tried turning his life around. But soon his religion became just a set of rules for him, rules that were then pushed onto his loved ones and onto society itself.

Now looking at him, I wonder what good that did him.

So where does that leave me? I contemplate the rise and fall of powerful things: people (like my father), cities (like Rome), and so on. Something so strong will eventually fall. If a society falls, it's a collective devastation but when a father falls, well, it's the most personal thing in the world...especially to a son.

So again, where does that leave me? It leaves me full of guilt though there was nothing I could have done to prevent the illness. But maybe I could have been a better son and maybe I still can but it's difficult for me to confront my father's condition. I'm so used to him being the person I go to for help even if, at times, I don't agree with his opinions. He was still there, still dependable. In my eyes, he knew almost everything.

What now?

A few months ago he suggested that he and I go to the movies together and I just sort of blew him off with the usual, "Yeah, sure, we can do that some time." But

I had no intention of doing it because I felt strange about going out in public with the man who was practically falling apart. I wasn't embarrassed for me but for him.

I don't know. I just have to watch the fall of Rome as it slowly slips into oblivion, an oblivion that will torture a son into submission but....submission to what? I don't want to fall back into his religion. I don't want to think that's the only way to connect to my father, to make peace with his disease. Will I feel at ease if I convert to his beliefs and huddle in prayer with him? There has to be another way.

Perhaps it's just a meaningless, random universe and the dice were thrown and landed in a way to push my father further down the road of pain and humiliation. I am only 31 years old and I find it somewhat unfair that my father is almost completely incapacitated. My own son cannot have the grandfather he deserves. My son finds my father to be scary and I know that breaks my father's heart and my own.

I don't know what this means for me.

It is the fall of Rome and I have to bear witness to it as it crumbles down, leaving everyone in the dust of blue collar work, religious dogma, forgotten dreams of musical stardom, and every other dream left undreamt. I am reduced to tears.

XVIII. SUPER ACTION BUILDING BLACK

Entry from *The Ultimate Anime Encyclopedia (2nd)* by Peter Myers:

XNOYBIS SUPER TERRORIST FORCE SIX

1992 / Dir: Chizuo Matsumoto / Writer: Murai Hideo / Translator: Henwich and Binger. 93 minutes. From the producers that brought us controversial anime films such as PENTEGRAM MOSK BLACK and ALL HAPPY FOUNDATION LSD comes this depressing and violent anime. Buildings in Tokyo come to life and wreak havoc. A special anti-terrorism task force is dispatched to deal with the problem. Things get worse when buildings all over the world start to revolt, blowing themselves up like monolith- ic suicide bombers. Add in Matsumoto and Hideo's trade- mark "black magic Buddhism" and tentacled-architecture monsters and you have one disturbing anime. This is also a subplot dealing with a shady corporation that resides inside one of the rogue buildings and is planning a worldwide biological attack. It's all a bit confusing but never gets boring. The ending in particular is depressing and existential. Not for the fainted hearted or easily upset. Note: There is a sequel (not yet available with English subtitles or dubbing) called SUPER XNOYBIS SUBWAY ATTACKING which was supposedly investigated by Japanese authorities for yet unexplained reasons.

XIX. HAPPY ENJOY HAPPINESS

Jessica sits in the hotel lobby. It is a major step for her. The swallowing of several of her pills has made it easier for her to deal with the crowd and all the people gawking at her.

The Taborica is running through her system.

She knows the people are gawking at her for who else would they be looking at?

They know about her father. They know about his suicide, about his jumping from a hotel window. Splat! A whole life snuffed out because of some pitiful human insecurities or untreated depression. Splat! A mother and daughter left alone to fend for themselves. Splat! Just another stain on the city sidewalk.

Those people, they must also know about the experiments. Jessica realizes that even if her dad wasn't a victim of the experiments, he might have been involved in it in some capacity. What if he was one of the victimizers? What if he had programmed some of the computers that were used in the experiments? She had read something about government scientists infecting homosexual men with AIDS in the early 1980s and that was about the time her father had worked for the government. Could it be that some of his computer work contributed to those sinister experiments? They weren't even experiments; they were exhibitions of atrocity and torture. It was some governmental game of sadomasochism and the politicians were too afraid to admit they got off on seeing gay men being infected and dying a slow death due to a virus that was completely and utterly man-made.

Had her father been involved in those experiments?

Jessica wonders about this and gets nervous. The people walking around the lobby of the hotel are eyeing her up even more now. One woman in particular (skinny black women in her fifties, shabbily dressed, filthy hair, but nice shoes) is staring at Jessica.

Jessica feels the pills soothe her nerves. She doesn't feel as worried. She feels as if she could handle the woman if she decides to confront her. She thinks about this and it becomes real.

"What do you know about my father?"

"Your father? Why would I know anything about your father?"

"You know damn well, you bitch. What do you know? Tell me now."

"Girl, you're crazy. I don't know your father from Adam and I think you must be on something for you to come up to a stranger and accuse them of something."

"I'm not accusing you of anything. I'm asking you straight out: what do you know about my father? I know you know something and I'm trying to get the details."

"Well, I don't have details for you. So get outta here before I beat your ass."

Jessica moves her face closer to the woman and spits.

"Liar!"

The black woman wipes the saliva from her face and grabs Jessica's hair. She says, "Oh, you want to know about your father? I'll tell you. He was a nutcase who couldn't keep his hands off the acid and electrodes, spent all his time jacking off to the white noise on the T.V. and anything on the news that had to do with bombs blowing shit up. He was a nutcase, girl, and if you had half a brain you'd get the hell out of the city before it explodes."

Jessica steps back from the lady because her breath smells like car exhaust. She walks backwards and trips over someone's luggage.

The ceiling appears over her head: a painting of a man falling out of a building, followed by others just like him: rejects from science, from government jobs, from LSD research and AIDS parties, bug-chasing physicists.

Jessica passes out.

XX. OUR GALAXIES ARE ERODING

Barry blames his impotence on the medication.

It makes sense being that sexual dysfunction was one of the side effects. But even with that in mind, his blaming of the medication didn't eliminate the stress. A part of him thinks he is somehow broken. It is a paranoid midlife crisis even though Barry is only thirty-one years old.

Barry decides to go into the city to check out a new aphrodisiac that's supposed to work great for his sort of problem. Normally he would never venture into the city but it was getting to the point where he couldn't satisfy his wife at all. It wasn't just a physical problem, it was a mental one. He cannot bring his mind to think about sex long enough for the blood to flow down to his crotch.

Something is getting in the way.

He walks into a public restroom and into a stall. He unbuttons his pants and takes out his flaccid penis. He stares at it. It's pitiful. It symbolizes the destruction of his masculinity. The medication he is taking might as well consist of microscopic terrorists that have destroyed Barry's great phallic tower.

Barry has the urge to punch himself in that area just out of spite. What would the medication-terrorists do then? Would they continue to bombard his body with microscopic bombs? Would they continue to destroy his manhood in other ways?

He is sure his wife is cheating on him. He doesn't blame her. If a husband cannot satisfy his wife sexually, then he isn't much of a husband. Barry just hopes she does not get emotionally involved with the man. Please let it be purely sexual. Please let it be purely for the purpose of satisfying her carnal needs. Please let the other man serve as an orgasm supplier and nothing more.

Barry thinks about this while staring down at his pale, floppy penis above the toilet in the public restroom.

He flushes the toilet and wishes his penis went down in the whirlpool. He fights the urge to tear into his body and pull out the remnants of the medication, those terrorist chemical-minerals that are creating chaos and havoc on his reproductive system.

He looks at the stall. It is covered in graffiti, mostly references to gangs and sexual acts. But there is something that catches Barry's eye. Written in thick black magic marker are the words NEVER FORGOT YOU ARE INVITED TO SUPREME TRUTH PARTY! HAPPY HA HA!

Barry leans his head against the words. "I'll be there," he says. He flushes the toilet and laughs.

XXI. SYNCRETIC SCOPOLAGNIA

No, I have never actually taken steps to commit what some have called *acts of terror*.

Yes, I have thought about techniques and strategies concerning these "acts of terror" but they were always kept in the realm of realistic fantasy, of a sterile examination of possibilities. I have considered myself a theoretical scientist of destructive fate.

No, I have never gathered bomb-making materials or anything that could be considered part of the explosive-making process. In fact, I wouldn't even know where to look for such things other than the Internet.

Yes, I have drawn up plans on how to create a scenario of mass death in a public place (a shopping mall) but it never passed the planning stages and was only a manifestation of my realistic fantasy of putting into action an experiment of destructive fate. It was all theory.

No, I did not buy guns or supplies specifically for this fantasy scenario. To go shopping for specific supplies would suggest *intent* and I had no intention of committing such "acts of terror" or anything else. I had a curiosity about these things and I satisfied this curiosity by planning.

Yes, I did bring a video camera to the shopping mall in order to document the path of my actors in this imaginary scenario. Like I said before, the videos were for research purposes only.

No, I don't hate people nor do I hate any country, state, province, town, et cetera. I am not political. I do not support or oppose any of the current hot-button social issues. I have no opinion on those things whatsoever. I am open to any and every viewpoint.

Yes, I recorded several hundred hours of footage on videocassette. I sell them to men I meet on the Internet. I became good friends with many of those men and arrange clandestine meetings with them at which we exchanged *information*.

No, I have never actually taken steps to commit what some have called *acts of terror*.

XXII. THE GYROVAGUES

At the core of my city, the fungal magnificence of the building enthralls me. It is majestic and borders on the holy. Automobiles and buses slow to let their occupants gasp or faint in ultraconscious worship of the monolithic tomb of the metropolis which is now swaying in the wind. I wave to the occupants but they do not wave back. Meditative pedestrians stalk the smoky streets while idly sipping their coffee and cursing the banality of their lives. I try to get their attention, try to explain my ideas for the expansion of panpsychism in every church, temple, mosque, and office building. The pedestrians do not listen. They start to scream. Their knees weaken; they fight the urge to fall to the sidewalk in supplication for to acquiesce so easily is a terrible transgression. They stare into the blue morning sky. They yearn to see the word of God. It is an important time for them.

It is the beginning of the new age.

Inside the basement, three men finish work copying several texts. One of them remarks how much the words look like "scribble-scrabble" and that makes him laugh. Though the cement room makes for an unconventional scriptorium, it is the only place the men could expect to complete their work without fear of interruption or infiltration. It is a psychic safe house, a bastion of textual security. It breathes when they breathe. It burps when they burp.

And now the three men are finished. Every syllable has been preserved. Every concept in many forms and incarnations has been documented. Every aspect of the texts is perfectly in sync with the originals.

It is the ending of a new age.

XXIII. GREAT AMERICAN NUDE NOVEL

Barry pulls a videocassette off the shelf: **Bloodfist VI: Ground Zero.**

He inserts it into the VCR and presses PLAY. He adjusts the tracking. He sits down in front of his typewriter.

The movie begins and Barry types along with the action and dialogue. He is integrating the plot of the movie into his own novel. He is not staying loyal to the story. On the contrary, he is adding much of his own imagination.

For example, he is including an alien race of beings that resemble skyscrapers who aid the terrorists in their mission. Barry knows it is a ridiculous plot device but he is obsessed with the idea of buildings as sentient beings, as destructive objects.

They are horrible things, these tall buildings, and Barry hates having to work in one. It is like having to work in a tomb. Everything about its architecture disgusts him and to come to some level of peace, Barry incorporates these feelings into his novel which he tentatively titles FALSE MAGIC KINGDOM.

He is not worried about his unlawful incorporation of the movie screenplay into his book. He doubts the writers or producers of the movie even remember what they made. Nor would they care to waste the legal fees in order to stop him from going through with publishing the book.

Barry feels safe in his endeavor. Besides, much of what he borrows is buried in his own prose, his own obscure words about evil buildings and shadowy corporations who have illicit dealings with a group of young Middle Eastern men who do nothing but plan things in the deserted offices in darkened skyscrapers.

Barry types.

Barry fills up ten pages and takes a break. He has a cigarette and thinks about his meeting with his boss.

Everything is going to hell. He feels pressured from every direction. His job. His wife. His book. Yes, even the book he is working on is pressuring him. He feels it tugging at his gut along with the nightmares of those skyscrapers, those ultrademonic buildings that sway in the wind and threaten to fall down on him, fall down into the streets, crushing traffic and spilling office jetsam into the sewers. He is writing the book not for enjoyment, not for fulfillment of a childhood dream but to escape from the never-ending daydreams of urban destruction.

The typewriter sits in front of Barry. It mocks him.

Barry leans back in his chair.

He feels an urge to punch the typewriter despite his affection for it. It is starting to remind him of an office building even though it doesn't resemble one in the least.

The telephone is to the right of the typewriter. Barry picks it up to call his cousin Tina. Perhaps he can confide in her. She has always been the stable one in the family.

XXIV. FATHERS

You must understand that I am not conceited. I am not too smart for my own good. I am not a know-it-all. I have considered myself a theoretical scientist of destructive fate. It is a way of being a part of society *without actually taking part in society.*

All experiments are a gift.

All experiments must be treated as such.

"If you know your party's extension, please. If you know your party's extension, please. If you know your party's extension, please.

Otherwise stay on the line to speak to a <static/white noise> bla…giraf…"

I'm not being paranoid.

Yes, yes you are. This always happens and I'm getting tired of dealing with it.

"So our government is sending out death squads?"

"Because of this possibility, I do not even entertain the idea of joining in their conversation to prove them wrong, to bring their ignorance to the forefront of their consciousnesses. I am a gentleman, really."

"Welcome to Pompeeeeeeeiiiiiiiiiiiiiiiiiiii…"

Every morning I wake up and my mouth is filled with the taste of dust and jet fuel. What do I do? What do I do to stop myself from drooling and babbling? I am an adult, yes, but I am also your child. I can't stop drooling.

"So what you want us to do? Not laugh when things are funny?"

"What do you know about my father?"

No, I have never actually taken steps to commit what some have called acts of terror.

NEVER FORGOT YOU ARE INVITED TO SUPREME TRUTH PARTY! HAPPY HA HA!

Thoughts are our own and as much as we want to think we control the thoughts, we cannot.

It is the ending of a new age. My father stutters and drools.

I am reduced to tears.

BAD ALCHEMY

A widespread taste for pornography means that nature is alerting us to some threat of extinction.
-J.G. Ballard

Dedicated to
Eckhart von Hochheim
and
Kirk Cameron

The thing is that you fall into it. For a long time the idea of writing has been appealing, maybe it is a question of self-expression, maybe only a sedentary way of pointing out to girls that you too have existence. Perhaps it has to do with the fact that something is bothering you and the only way that you can take it to terms is to get it down on paper, usually in a lying kind of way that may have to do, in the long run, with truth...

-Barry Malzberg

A.M.

Automobiles explode. No one has read the roadside announcements. There is no parking here. There is no parking anywhere. The situation is too dangerous. Just yesterday a judge's car was blown into fiery bits, killing a handful of innocent people who had the misfortune of wanting an autograph or an appeal.

So today is really just like any other day. Perhaps it is a bit tenser, filled with more anxiety for all those who venture out into the labyrinthine city but there is still hope in the perpetual work ethic of most people.

The buildings sway slightly in the wind. If you look closely, you can see them and it is truly frightening. Any minute they could sway just a little too much and come crashing down like the blocks of rowdy children.

What will fall next? I imagine it will be the sun. The sun will come crashing down in a last ditch effort to prove the dominance of Sol Invictus. But I imagine the workday will go on. People will adapt to the change. They will show great resolve. They are hard-working people, after all.

Get dressed. It is the beginning of the work day.

*

Three women use computers to enter the data. They double and triple check each other's work. They print out copies of the data and place them in filing cabinets. They lock the filing cabinets and enter more data into the computers.

Each tap of the keyboard and click of the mouse brings a distinct code, an aural trigger that is vital to the women's work day. The clicks and clattering form music that forces the women to tap along with their high-heeled feet.

Incarnations of their data digitally transform into incantations of knowledge and blueprints of future projects. They are projects for the ages, for the betterment of mankind, womankind, and humankind.

The women click-clack their high-heels in a rapid cacophony.

They type.

They click-clack.

They type.

As noon approaches, the women stand up at their desks and stretch, revealing the sweat stains under their arms.

The bell rings.

It's lunchtime.

Part of the public horror of sexual irregularity so-called is due to the fact that everyone knows himself essentially guilty.
-Aleister Crowley

I. HAPPY FUNTIME USA

Barry opens his wallet, checks his money situation, and walks into the small shop.

Hideo Video.

He had passed it a few times over the last few months but had never gone inside. He had always thought it too small and crowded and besides, everything in there was Japanese. It was a culture clash he wasn't interested in experiencing. He felt too ignorant to even try.

But a few days ago something had caught his eye: a large poster of a burning building. Brightly colored Japanese words surround the building but at the bottom in pink letters were words in English: NEVER FORGOT YOU ARE INVITED TO SUPREME TRUTH PARTY! HAPPY HA HA!

Smiley faces floating around the destruction. A kitty cat hanging out of a window, waving. Something about it intrigues Barry. He wants to know what the poster is advertising. A band? A television show? A new food? A comic? A movie? A pornographic movie?

After a few days of slowly walking past the store to stare at the poster, he finally decides to go inside. So Barry checks his wallet and walks into the small shop.

Hideo Video.

It is a sensory overload of posters of all shapes, sizes, and colors along with figurines, video tapes, toys, cassette tapes, pillows, novelty candy, costumes, and other colorful jetsam. Music is playing: fast-paced pop music with high-pitched vocals of a manic little girl singing in childish Japanese.

Barry spins around slowly. He cannot digest it all, cannot process everything. Dizziness sets in but a voice lulls him to safety.

"Help you?" a middle-aged Japanese man says, standing up from behind the glass counter which is filled with small toy robots and humanoid figurines.

Barry makes eye contact with the man but says nothing. He wonders if he should ask about the poster. But would that seem strange? Is it strange that an American walks into the store to buy a poster of something he knows nothing about?

"Just browsing," Barry replies.

"What?" the man says, coming around the counter to get close to Barry. "What do you mean browsing?"

"Just looking around." Barry slowly moves his body for a quick getaway. He immediately regrets having walked into the shop.

"What do you want? What do you need?" The man's accent is diminishing.

"Uh, I'm not sure, I mean, I'm just looking."

"You like movies?"

"Yeah, I…"

"Come, come," the Japanese man says, grabbing Barry's shoulder and gently leading him to the back of the store where there is a large bookcase with hundreds of VHS tapes. All were in Japanese. "See something you like?"

"To be honest, I just came in here because I saw that poster." Barry points across the store to the wall above the counter. "I like it."

"Oh, yes yes yes!"

Barry is startled by the man's response.

"Yes! Yes! Come here, come here, let me show you!" The Japanese man walks over to the poster and stares at it proudly. "This is poster for movie. New, very nice."

"What movie?"

"Yes, yes! I have a copy. Wait!" The Japanese man bends down and rummages through boxes under the counter. He stands and proudly holds up a large VHS case. It has the same art as the poster. There is a piece of white paper taped to the corner with crude handwriting that says: XNOYBIS SUPER TERRORIST FORCE SIX.

"You want?" the man says.

Barry remembers the money in his wallet. He had originally only wanted to purchase the poster. He wasn't interested in the actual movie. "What is it?"

"Ah, movie, you like it. Very exciting, action, things go BOOM," the man says, clapping his hands. "Pretty girls, tough men, evil demons, guns, buildings. BOOM!" The man claps again but this time very close to Barry's face. "Family movie."

Barry flinches. He catches a whiff of seafood from the man's fingers.

"How much?" Barry says.

"Fifty for movie plus poster."

"How much for just the poster?"

"No! I sell as set."

Barry grabs his wallet, fingers the faux-leather for a second, and decides to give in to the pressure. "Okay."

As the man bags the VHS tape and rolls up the poster, Barry looks at the items on display in the glass counter. Aside from the robot toys, there are cassette tapes, minimally labeled and clearly displayed:

SWISSAIR 1970
REGGIO 1970
LOD AIRPORT 1972

NUCLEI ARMATI RIVOLUZIONARI 1980
BANCO DE VIZCAYA 1983
KIM HYON HUI 1987
SUITCASE UT-772 1989
HAPPY SUBWAY MARCH 1995
OK CITY, OK! HAPPY 1995

The last tape catches Barry's eye. Behind it is a book-let with the words YOU BEEN WILL HAPPY, TOO in thick but faded black letters and a lopsided smiley face.

"Oh, you looking for music, too, eh?" the Japanese man says. "Those cassettes, those you can't find anywhere else in New York. They come straight from Japan. You want?"

"What are they?"

"Sounds."

"Music?"

"Sounds!" The Japanese man claps his hands in front of Barry's face again.

"What kind of sounds? I mean, what kind of music?"

"Oh! Not like rock and roll. These are sounds, boom, bang, sounds of life, sounds of the living and the sounds of….Boom! Very happy sounds. Loud sounds. Make you very happy."

"Um, what about that one? OK CITY…..?"

"Oh, is good one. Comes with book, too."

"How much?"

"Thirty."

"Oh…"

"Too much? I make you deal. Give you movie, poster, and cassette, all for sixty-five. Deal?"

Barry looks at the nondescript cassette and the booklet behind it. He is intrigued. "Okay, I'll take it."

"Good! Good!" The man goes into the counter and grabs the cassette and booklet. He puts them into the same bag with Barry's movie. He grabs another cassette behind him and replaces it in the counter. This one says: BEIRUT 1983 (2 TAPES)

The man hands the bag to Barry with one hand while taking the money with the other.

"Enjoy! Have happy day!"

Barry nods. "Thank you. You too."

While he leaves, Barry hears the man clap loudly.

"Boom!"

II. BUILDING BLACK PYRAMIDS

Tina walks into the Atrax Institute and asks the receptionist if Dr. Sotos is available.

"We don't accept walk-ins," the receptionist says with a heavy Italian accent.

"But it's important. I have a referral from Dr. Corbelli."

"Well, Dr. Corbelli doesn't usually do that, you know. Hold on." The receptionist stands up and walks into the backroom, leaving Tina to stand conspicuously in the waiting room surrounded by outdated art on the walls and even more outdated magazines on the chairs.

A minute later, the receptionist returns. Behind her is a skinny, pale man in a doctor's coat. There are dark circles around his eyes. He says, "I am Dr. Corbelli. You say I referred you?"

Tina cringes. She has told a lie. "Well, I…."

"Where did you get my name?"

"I heard this is the place to go for what I need."

"And what is it that you need?"

"I need help."

"What kind of help?" the pale doctor walks towards Tina.

She feels the coldness of his skin as he puts his face close to hers, waiting for an answer.

"I need surgery."

"What kind of surgery?"

Tina glances at the nurse and then back at the doctor. "Can we talk about this in private?"

"I suppose so. But Dr. Sotos is not here if that's who you came for."

"Well…I was told he was the…specialist."

Both Dr. Corbelli and the receptionist laugh. "Oh, yes, he is a specialist!"

Tina smiles nervously.

"Well, what is your name?"

"Tina."

"Tina what?"

"Tina Bayley."

"We have some papers for you to fill out and then we can discuss whether or not we can help you."

Tina nods and takes a clipboard the receptionist hands her. Dr. Corbelli retreats back through the door from which he came and Tina is left alone in the waiting room. She stares down at the questionnaire.

Name. Date of Birth. Social Security Number. Name of Insurance Company. Policy Number. Name of Employer. Phone Number of Employer.

Tina fills out what she can. She leaves the insurance information blank. She hopes she can come to some sort of arrangement.

She flips to the next page.

Do you have a history of sexual dysfunction? Have you or anyone in your immediate family ever had a sexually transmitted disease? On average, how many times do you have intercourse in a month? When having intercourse, how long does it usually take you (on average) to reach orgasm? Are your orgasms accompanied by nightmares or waking dreams? If you answered yes, do these dreams involve any of the following: grotesque food products, office buildings, gelatinous substances, airplanes, supermarkets, giraffes with unusual coloring, obscure religious symbology? Have you ever inserted a foreign object into your vagina/urethra/anus? Have you ever consumed bodily fluid (blood, semen, mucous) other than your own? If so, how much and how often? Do you suffer from delusions? Do you suffer from an overactive bladder? Do you suffer from an irritable bowel? And lastly…..

Reason for visit?

Tina answers the questions but she leaves a few blank.

The receptionist walks in and takes the clipboard from Tina.

"You didn't answer all of them," she says.

"Yeah, um, I wasn't sure what to answer."

"The questions are pretty simple. Like…have you inserted a foreign object into your vagina or anus? That is a simple yes or no. Do you have a memory problem as well?"

"Can't I just speak to the doctor about this?"

The receptionist sighs. "You are not making it easy for me to help you. All information must be filled out or else the doctor won't even consider seeing you." She hands Tina back the clipboard.

Tina takes it and reluctantly fills in the rest.

The receptionist says, "You can go in now." She leads Tina down the hallway and into room number three. "The doctor will be with you in a moment."

Tina nods and is about to ask a question but the door is shut and she is left alone again.

The wallpaper is ancient: pictures of cartoon patients smiling while cartoon doctors examine them with old-fashioned instruments. Tina sits on the examining table and gets a closer look at the yellowing pictures.

Tina wonders about the cartoon doctors. Yes, they are just cartoons but they look so happy to be taking care of their patients. The patients themselves look overjoyed to be there. Tina has never had an experience with a doctor that made her feel so much satisfaction.

So now what?

She doesn't know what to expect from Dr. Corbelli or Dr. Sotos. She knows they specialize in certain procedures that involve her type of...problem but that is all. Whether or not they are good doctors, she does not know.

Tina leans her head against the wallpaper and closes her eyes.

The door to the examining room opens and in walks Dr. Corbelli.

He says, "After looking over your medical history, I'm a bit concerned."

"Concerned about what?"

"What exactly do you want us to do? You do know the Atrax Institute specializes in...certain procedures..."

"I know."

"But you weren't very specific here on the questionnaire. I'd like to know a detailed explanation of what your problem is and how you think we can help you."

Tina stutters through an introduction to her problem but her tongue swells and her throat constricts. Finally, she pulls down her pants and panties, letting her two penises hang out.

Dr. Corbelli's head drops, his eyes never leaving Tina's crotch. He moans and says, "I see the problem...and I see the solution."

"So you can help me?"

Dr. Corbelli claps his hands. "Of course!"

III. FANTASY FOOTAGE OF AIRLINE ABUSE

Not gonna split hairs here!

A victim is a victim is a victim and a hole is a hole is a hole. That's what I've learned and that's what I'm saying to you all now. When I say "you all" I really just mean you because, let's face it, only one person is going to be reading this at a time. I don't imagine my little scribble-scrabble is going to make it into some sort of book club or be read aloud at a funeral or something.

So I'm not gonna split hairs, I'm not gonna beat around the bush and all that. I'm a victim, okay? I said it.

That's the first step and I said it loud and clear for you all ("you all" haha!) to hear. I'm a victim but guess what? So are you.

We're the same: me and you, you and him, she and I, etc. Just victims but we are no more victims than anyone else. Know what else we are? Meat manikins cursed with the gift of movement and sometimes even foresight.

How's that for an imaginative criticism of humanity!

God, I'm sounding like a morose jerk, aren't I? I admit that I've taken a few psychology courses at the local university (okay, community college) and I like to ponder these things, dissect them, approach reality in a way that's different than anyone else's approach. Those classes have left me a little critical of humanity. That's what college does to a person, makes them cold and critical.

I am sitting in a stall of the college bathroom and while looking at all the juvenile graffiti about body parts and phone numbers, I decide I am just a lump of flesh with a hole at the bottom and am waiting for stuff to exit that hole. That's the simple set-up. Are you all still with me?

I hear a roar outside.

The windows are frosted or something so I can't see out. But the windows rattle and sound like they are about to shatter. I don't have to tell you all that I am pretty terrified. No one wants to be stuck on the toilet during some sort of an emergency and at this point, I have no idea of the nature of that emergency. For all I know it could be the end of the world, the Second Coming, an erupting volcano, an earthquake, a hurricane or something. I know all of that is unrealistic but when startled like that, many things will go through one's mind.

I put my eyes to the frosted glass and feel the rattling against my eyelids. It tickles and feels sort of nice. Through the glass I can't really see much. Just some shapes, some shadows, and…something.

The glass is still rattling and my eyelids keep being tickled and I must admit I am feeling pretty good considering something major could be happening right on the other side of this frosted glass.

I hear the door of the restroom open and footsteps tip-toe to the stall next to me. Someone slowly lifts the toilet seat and starts to urinate. Are they not hearing the commotion outside?

"Hello?" I ask. "Know what's going on out there?"

"Shhh!" the guy says, continuing to urinate.

"You don't hear that?"

"Shhh!"

So I shush. I'm not in the mood to make trouble. I figure something is happening outside and it will do me no good to start a fracas inside the men's room at the community college.

The toilet next to me flushes and the man tip-toes out of the bathroom without stopping to wash his hands. That sort of bothers me, actually. I don't expect him to sit there and scrub his hands raw but it's common courtesy to at least wet your hands when you urinate even if you only touched your penis (which may very well be clean but that's not really the point, now, is it?).

The noise outside is growing louder, the glass rattles more violently, and my eyelids flicker like crazy until the light coming through the frosted glass throws light/shadow shapes into my brain.

What's out there? A zeppelin? Something like that. Or a space shuttle? Something like that. Maybe a zeppelin, yes, that's what I think because I imagine being in the nineteenth century and being in awe at the new flying machines and whatnot. That's what I am thinking about. That is my thought pattern. I think about H.G. Wells for some reason even though I don't think I actually ever read anything by him. That's one of my confessions:

I've never read a thing by H.G. Wells.

The glass is still rattling and the shadow/light show gets more intense until my face is basically glued to the frosted glass.

I tear myself away, pull up my pants, and leave the bathroom to go outside and investigate.

And yes, I wash my hands before I leave.

IV. SCRIBBLE SCRABBLE

Jessica passes out.

She dreams about bombs, about buildings, about rental vans, about breaking bread with strangers, drinking weak wine with those same strangers who turn out not to be strangers at all but some of her classmates from high school. They are in her bedroom. They are snorting Ritalin, Luvox, Taborica, and paroxetine. They talk about rifles, which one is best, which one looks better, which one won't be missed, which one they can order through the mail.

They discuss "primal assassins" yet they have no idea what that means. One of them has read it in a book once. They giggle. They snort again and Jessica's father walks into the room. Jessica is shocked. Hadn't her father killed himself when she was nine years old?

"What are you girls doing?" he says.

"Nothing, dad. Nothing. Just talking."

"Looks like you're doing more than talking," he says.

"What's that stuff on the book over there?"

"What stuff?" Jessica wishes someone would sneeze and make the pill-dust go away. She tries to move the copy of A Brief History of Industrial Parks to the edge of the bed so it will fall and let the pill-dust hide in the shag carpet.

Her father walks over, looks down at the powder covered book and scoffs. "You know, I can't believe this..."

"I'm sorry, dad."

"Sorry, yeah, I know you are," her father says. "You know what? I should have killed myself years ago."

Jessica bursts into tears. Her friends are still and

speechless. They are simply props, pill-fueled manikins.

"Dad!" Jessica says, lunging forward. She wraps her arms around his legs.

"Stop, Jess. You're embarrassing me."

"But Dad!"

"I'm going to watch T.V. now. Tell your friends to leave and then clean this mess up."

Jessica feels the floor give way. The ceiling follows her into the basement. She hits cement, sinks into it, sinks into the earth, watches her father stare at the white noise, his hand down his pants, and electrodes buzzing on his skull as he watches funny suicides on the television.

V. STRUCTURES

Someone left a bunch of Xeroxed pictures around the office.

I walk out of the bathroom and seem them scattered on the floor and crudely taped to the walls. The pictures are all the same: a grainy black-and-white reproduction of an architectural blueprint.

Everyone in the office is at the window, their noses mashed up on the glass, looking out at something with their eyes all wide and their mouths gaping. What the hell are they looking at? I'm always late to things. I always miss out. For once I'd like to be included in something.

I don't want to continue to be the odd woman out so I join them. That's all I need: for someone to start a rumor and say they saw me in the corner, not joining in, not being part of the team. I don't want people to think I'm a snob or standoffish. Yes, I'm shy, but I truthfully like my coworkers and want to be included.

With my nose mashed up against the warm glass, I look out the window. Now I know why someone left those Xeroxed pictures around the office. And I thank them for it.

VII. ANTIOCHUS IV EPIPHANES CC / BCC

"Okay, Ronald, you can have a seat," says Samuel Mathers.

"Thank you, sir."

"You know why you're here, right?"

"Not exactly, no."

"The Barry situation."

"Oh yes, of course."

"And?"

"Uh, I had a meeting with him yesterday."

"And….?"

"It's in the process of being settled."

"I don't like processes, Ronald. I like results, solutions. Final solutions. Not processes. Not ongoing processes. I don't like waiting. I don't like processes."

"I know. I'm sorry. I'll take care of it ASAP."

"Do I need to assign this to someone else?"

"No, I can handle it."

"How long have you been with this company?"

"Uh, a little over ten years."

"Do you think you are as qualified today as you were ten years ago?"

"I've actually been here a little more than ten years ago. Closer to eleven."

"Do you think you are as qualified today as you were a little more than ten years ago, closer to eleven?"

"Yes, even more so."

"What makes you believe that?"

"Well, I…," says Ronald, gasping for air.

"Do you need to go get a drink of water?"

"No, I'm fine."

"You said you're more than qualified. How so?"

"I…I mean, just the experience alone makes me more qualified."

"Are you saying we are not using you to your full potential? Are you saying we should get someone else less qualified than you for this task?"

"Uh, no, I mean, I don't know what you're…I do my job well, sir."

"Maybe too well. You just said you're overqualified."

"That's not what I meant."

"You should always say what you mean, Ronald."

"I know, I…"

"Are you or are you not dissatisfied with this task or with your employment as a whole? I can't have feelings of discontent contaminating the workplace."

"I am perfectly happy with my job, sir."

"Job? That's all this is? A job? A job is something someone has when they are too lazy to train for a career."

"I am perfectly happy with my career, sir. I am one-hundred percent comfortable and qualified."

"That's what I thought. You're comfortable in your position. You are so comfortable, in fact, that things aren't getting done. Everything is a process with you, Ronald. I don't like processes. I like results, solutions. Final solutions. Not processes. Not ongoing processes. I don't like waiting. I don't like processes."

"I know, sir…"

"I'm constantly waiting for this mythical event called ASAP but have yet to experience it. What does ASAP mean to you, Ronald?"

"With all due respect, sir…"

"No, stop talking."

"But I…"

"We're done."

"But…"

"You can leave now, Ronald. You can leave."

VIII. MECHANICAL FOLKLORE

First, it didn't happen like that at all, no way. Through an adult version of the telephone game, law enforcement and the media have deformed the truth in such a way as to make it unrecognizable. Now it's a different entity altogether. It is a foreign concept. It is false. It is an untruth, almost a myth, an exaggerated version of a parody.

Second, even if it did happen like that (and as I stated above, it most certainly did not) I would have been justified in my actions because when we come down to it, a person needs to accept his or her position in society and act accordingly. Not everyone can do what their neighbor can nor should they be expected to try just for the appeasement of the rest of society.

Third, I can't be expected to accept the judgment simply based on the "facts" and can't be expected to sit quietly while others dissect my situation, deform my words, constructing (and deconstructing) them into highly controversial information so much so that I am slowly beginning to despise myself based on their findings.

Fourthly, let's look at the phrase "acts of terror" and its connotations. There is no way to spin that into a positive light without totally reconstructing the situation and the perceptions held by all the participants and the audience (the public). Therefore, all phraseology is subjective and persecutory. Notice how I put "acts of terror" in quotes and that's how it should be. When you read that, you know I am being sarcastic or ironic or something that proves that I do not take that phrase seriously when used in connection with my own situation. By using quotes, I am taking control over the situation.

"My" actions, meaning that I did not have sole ownership of said actions, are a result of a chain of causation ("chain" of causation?) and my subsequent "persecution" by the "journalists" who have written "articles" about my "situation" and "acts of terror" has lead to my moral, physical, psychic, sexual, and mental "disintegration" which has contributed to my current "unfortunate" situation.

Finally, please wait until you pass judgment on "me" as it will only serve society better. Maybe I should put "society" in quotes.

Everything, including society, is hypothetical.

IX. OK CITY, OK! HAPPY 1995 SIDE ONE

Barry goes to the stereo and puts in the tape he bought from Hideo Video, and presses PLAY.

Tape hiss and then….an engine. A truck engine? Muffled voices, rubber hitting asphalt, machine hums, more voices, tapping, jingling.

A pause…a few seconds of silence. Next song?

More engine sounds, frantic, loud, the bass over-whelms everything else. The speakers on Barry's tape recorder sound like they are about to burst open in analog destruction. He lowers the volume just a tad.

A voice on the tape says, "Pull it."

Door slams, more voices, another door slams, a single voice laughing. There's a boom and then a BOOM. Crashing metal, hissing, voices. Door slams.

Tape hiss gets loud, louder than the sounds on the tape. Barry is afraid the cassette is going to break in the player but then the hiss dies down and the engine sound begins again. Then:

Voices.

Silence.

Tape hiss.

A high pitched whistling.

Hands clapping.

Cheers.

A muffled voice says, "Boom."

It is the end of side one.

X. FISHERS OF MEN

My grandfather was a blue collar worker, doing his time at a General Motors factory, I believe. He was a Mets fan much to the dismay of my father, a Yankees fan. I always wondered if my father had become a Yankees fan out of some sort of rebellion or spite.

My grandfather also hunted and fished which always struck me as odd because my father did neither. Maybe it wasn't strange. Maybe my father just decided to not participate in those things in order to distance himself from his own father. I don't know. I never asked him. Maybe, like being a Yankees fan, it was my father's way of rebelling.

When I was about 7 or 8 years old, the subject came up about a fishing trip with all three of us. Being a normal little boy, it was something I wanted very much: to participate in manly activities with my paternal role models. I remember their talking about having to wake up early (earlier than I'd ever woken up) and so on. I was excited.

A fishing trip!

But it never happened. I never went fishing. Not then, not ever.

I don't know why it never happened. I have a feeling my father backed out of it or found some excuse why it wasn't a good idea. Maybe my grandfather wanted to do it on a Sunday and you know, that was the Lord's Day according to my father.

I'm not resentful but I feel bad for myself as that young boy eager to bond with my father and grandfather. A part of me feels like this is a failure on my dad's part and if so, I wonder: will I fail in the same way with my own child?

But I've realized an important fact: everybody fails.

This is no escaping it. Everyone is a failure.

That's not to say I'll give up. No. I am many things but I'm not a pessimist or fatalist. Pessimism is for lazy, bitter people who lack the self-confidence to attempt to change their lives.

So, yes, everybody fails. I'm a failure but so is everyone else. We are all on the same level when it comes down to it. Readjusted failures and new perspectives will turn the negatives into positives. Get it?

So now I switch this narrative and address my child: I will do my best not to fail you in a way that will leave you disappointed. You must accept that I will fail you sometimes but maybe just the same as everyone else and perhaps the level of failure will be overshadowed by my love and the other things I do.

But I don't know the first thing about fishing. If it is something you really want to do, I'm sure I can learn. We can't expect Grandpa to join us because of his condition but you and I will have fun anyway. Then you can tell Grandpa all about it. A part of me hopes he will feel bad for not taking me fishing but that would not be my predominant motive in having you tell him about it.

So bottom line: probably no fishing but definitely some failures. No hunting, but some good memories together nonetheless.

Everybody fails so...that's it. We're all failures. That's what I learned from not going fishing.

XI. WINDOW WASHER

Bunting zooms in, pans to the left, and focuses the camera on the building's 93rd floor. Sunlight reflects off the glass, blinds him for a few seconds.

"Ugh!" he says.

"What?" Jali says.

"Light."

"What?"

"The light."

"So what?"

"Blinded me."

"So what?"

"Ugh," Bunting says. He looks back into the camera and squints. He wishes the zoom was stronger. He wishes he could somehow move upwards on an invisible elevator or flying carpet to get a better view.

REC.

The camera is recording.

"Go down a few floors," says Jali.

"How many?"

"A few."

"What? Two, three, four?"

"Do it!"

Bunting grunts and dramatically moves the camera down, pointing it at the third floor.

Jali slams his fist down. "I said a few!"

"Oops." Bunting tilts the camera upwards to the 88th floor.

"Bam. Boom! To the moon!" Jali says, slapping his hands together.

Bunting shakes his head. "That's all we need. Footprints on the moon."

"Soon, skeletons on the moon."

"That's absurd, Jali."

"Not as absurd as you think."

"What do you…?"

"Boom!"

"What?"

"We have lift-off!" Jali claps his hands.

Bunting zooms out.

XII. AN INTRODUCTION BY WALTER MARTIN

There are plenty of journalists who would decline the offer to interview the MAN because, let's face it: nothing good could really come out of interviewing HIM. Every interview ever attempted, whether it be for print or for television, has ended in disaster for either the journalist or the entire publication/network. No one really thinks it's necessarily a curse as much as it's the MAN subtly (and sometimes not so subtly) putting into place latent sparks of causation, tiny fingers pushing multiple dominos until they all start falling. Everything he touches ends in some dark obscure perversion, split open like rotted wood to reveal ruined faces humiliated by mold and truth.

But enough with the melodramatics: this is serious business.

I am the only journalist who is willing to sit down with the MAN, across from the MAN, and ask the questions, tackle the topics, dare to delve into things no one has had the courage to do before. I will stare the MAN in the face and seek the TRUTH.

But please don't think I'm trying to present myself as some sort of media hero or pioneer. I'm just a man trying to get the TRUTH to the people while also getting the story of my career. There's nothing wrong with gaining a little something while doing the right thing, now, is there?

I think that's the American way and I'm proud to follow that path. I'll follow that path to the MAN and to the TRUTH. You just wait and see.

XIII. INVOCATION BLIND IDIOT LIBIDO

"What the hell are you listening to?" Barry's wife says.

"Oh, nothing. Just a tape…"

"Tape? You mean like a cassette tape?"

"Yeah."

"Why?"

"Just something I picked up at the store. Looked interesting," Barry says, worried what his wife will think. He's embarrassed. Who listens to cassettes nowadays? His wife must think he's an idiot.

"What is it?" she says. "Sounds like noise."

"That's what it is, I guess."

"You paid money for that?"

Barry nods and hopes she doesn't ask how much.

"How much?" his wife says.

"Not much."

She sighs. It is not a disgruntled sigh. It is a sigh of pity and love.

Barry feels like he should make a move. They hadn't made love in months but lord knows they've tried. He stands up and touches her shoulder. "You want to…do stuff?"

"We can try," she says, giving him a kiss. "Think you're up to it?" She giggles innocently.

Barry blushes and smiles. "I hope so." But he is not so sure. His penis is a bloodless, inanimate object, a phallic idol of some distant civilization that had existed earlier in the marriage but has since disappeared and is forgotten like a religion-turned-myth.

Barry stares at the cassette player as his wife tries her best to bring the idol to life but it is to no avail. The tape hiss mocks his impotence.

Finally he stops her. "Forget it. I don't think it's going to happen. I'm sorry."

"There's nothing to be sorry about. It's just your medication."

"I know. I just feel…you know…"

"It's okay, hon." She kisses him.

The tape hiss grows louder, grows into a rumbling, grows into small bursts of pink noise, into a pulsating tone, voices, doors slamming and then:

"Pull it."

BOOM.

XIV. AN INTERVIEW BY WALTER MARTIN

WALTER: First, let me thank you for the interview.

MAN: You don't have to thank me, Walter.

WALTER: A lot of people, journalists in particular, think you are a horrible man. Do you know that some people have expressed this sentiment?

MAN: I am aware, yes.

WALTER: And it doesn't bother you?

MAN: No. Should it?

WALTER: It would bother most people.

MAN: Well, I'm not most people.

WALTER: I just want to make clear that I personally do not hold to that opinion.

MAN: I wouldn't care if you did, Walter.

WALTER: Have other people's opinions had any effect on your past actions?

MAN: Their opinions only affect how they see my past actions. But I don't think that's what you're asking. In the past, their opinions did not matter to me, no. I'm not a vindictive man. My actions aren't those of….what did they say? Oh yes, terror, acts of terror. They were not acts of terror. That's such a loaded word: terror. It holds so much historical, emotional weight. Terror! Actions are neutral events until people start labeling them. Their opinions about me and the…situation were already formed before anything happened.

WALTER: And the most recent incident?

MAN: Incident. That's a funny word. When it is in their best interest, the media will call certain events "incidents" even when such an event is a massacre of biblical proportions. If it's in their best interest, they may call a nearly identical event a "tragedy" but again, that's only when it suits them. Incident or not, what do you want to know about it? I don't believe I understand the question.

WALTER: I think what everyone wants to know is...why?

MAN: Why what, Walter? Why did it happen? It happened because all the parts were in place: physically, economically, politically, psychically, socially, even sexually. There was no way it was not going to happen, Walter.

WALTER: Let's be honest. That sounds like a lot of doubletalk, like you want to fill the airtime with words but not really divulge anything relevant. You are not giving me any specific details.

MAN: You want specific details? Then ask specific questions, Walter. You're asking amateur questions in the hopes that I'll be eager enough to spill everything here on the soapbox you've provided me. You don't have the guts to actually ask the right questions. You thought getting the interview was enough to prove your worth as a journalist but you're wrong. You're a coward, Walter. Your audience sees it. I see it. But most importantly, you see it.

WALTER: There is no need to resort to personal attacks. I'm trying to conduct a professional interview here and you're getting out of line.

MAN: The word professional holds no meaning when speaking about the media.

WALTER: Do you want to end this interview?

MAN: No. Do you?

WALTER: I just want to conduct a....serious interview.

MAN: Then ask a serious question.

WALTER: Do you feel directly responsible for the deaths?

MAN: No.

WALTER: Do you feel indirectly responsible for the deaths?

MAN: No.

WALTER: Do you feel at least partially responsible for the deaths?

MAN: Everyone is partially responsible for the deaths.

WALTER: How so?

MAN: It would take hours for me to explain the chain of causation and even if we had the time, and even if I was willing to give you the time, which I am not, you would not be able to understand nor would your audience.

WALTER: There is no need to insult my audience.

MAN: Your audience?

WALTER: Yes, my audience. This show is quite popular. There are a lot of good people tuning in so let's keep this respectful.

MAN: Get on with your interview, then.

WALTER: Your attitude towards the media is very hostile. Why is that?

MAN: Ask a serious question.

WALTER: That is a serious question. You have an axe to grind against my colleagues and me. Why?

MAN: You want me to like you? You want me to like your colleagues? Do you need me to like you? Is that what this interview was for? You wanted my acceptance? My friendship? I didn't agree to this interview in order to con- sole your bruised ego.

WALTER: This is no ego here. I simply represent the media.

MAN: You?

WALTER: Yes, me.

MAN: What have you done to earn that position, Walter?

WALTER: I don't have to explain…

MAN: Have your colleagues, your peers, agreed to such a representation? Have they voted on it? Have they held meetings to discuss your qualifications as minimal as they might be? I wasn't aware I was in the presence of a representative of such stature.

WALTER: Listen. You have no…

MAN: I will not listen to the howling of dogs!

WALTER: You're insane.

MAN: Ask a serious question.

WALTER: This interview is over.

XV. YOU CAN HAVE ANYTHING YOU WANT

Entry from *The Mega Guide to Children's Films* by Peter Myers:

THE ADVENTURES OF XNOYBIS PART 6

1971/ Dir: Mark Corbelli / Writers: Mark Corbelli and Donald Sotos / 93 minutes. From the producers that brought us micro-budget talking animal films such as LE ROUX THE DONKEY and DUCK, DUCK, MOOSE? comes this confusing yet strangely entertaining film. A young boy named Danny explores the basement of his father's office building and stumbles upon an old albino who educates the boy in the ways of white magic. The two encounter sinister Aladdin-like thieves, mysterious corporate assassins, magical creatures, and an evil wizard who just happens to be connected to Danny's father. With bad dubbing (the voices were redone in post-production) and bad editing, this is a mess of a film but it makes for engaging viewing. This was to be the last film of the writing team of Corbelli and Sotos before they disappeared into obscurity.

XVI. FULL DISCLOSURE

Once a day: 10 MG. Paxil
Once a day: 5 MG. Vesicare
Once a day: .5 MG. Domedon
Once a day: 5 MG. Doxomedon
Twice a day: 10 MG. Taborica
Twice a day: .25 MG. Hyoscyamine
Twice a day: 4 MG. Imodium
Twice a day: 1 MG. Klonopin

XVII. YOU SHOULD SEE A DOCTOR

Ronald comes home to his wife looking through his work papers.

"What are you doing?" he says.

"Looking for evidence."

"Evidence of what?"

"Did you know in 1973, your company made several business deals with a subsidiary of Atrax International?'

"No. Should I?"

"Atrax International was responsible for…"

"Susan, I don't want to hear it," Ronald says. "Did you take your meds today?"

"Ron, did you hear what I just said?"

"Did you take your meds?"

"Did you have a meeting with your boss today, Ron?"

"Yeah…how did you know?"

"Someone called and told me."

"What are you talking about? Who called you?"

"Someone. They didn't tell me who they were."

"What exactly did they say?"

"They said, 'Ronald will be talking to Samuel today.'"

"That's it?"

"Yes, that was it. Then they hung up."

"What the hell is going on? Is that why you're going through my stuff ?"

"No. I'm going through your stuff to see if I can find any evidence."

"You're being ridiculous, Susan."

"Am I?"

"Yes," Ronald says. "And you didn't answer my question. Did you take your meds?"

"So you're a part of this, too, I guess."

"Part of what, Susan?"

"It...part of it." Her eyes widen. She backs away from Ronald.

"I think we need to call Dr. Visna."

"No!"

"I think you need to talk to someone."

"Just let me finish looking."

"Listen, Susan…"

"Leave me alone!"

"Susan…" Ronald steps towards his wife and she backs away. She trips over a box of papers. She falls and lands on her behind.

"Get away from me!"

"I'm calling the doctor."

"No! I don't need any help!"

"The hell you don't."

Susan starts pulling papers out of the box, sending them into the air. She throws a handful at Ronald and crawls out of the room on her hands and knees. She closes the door behind her. From the other room she screams.

"Death squads!"

XVIII. DEVILS BY THE DEED

So with this, my report of the events, a report I will be sending to no one but myself, I seek to justify my action (or non-action) during the months of April and May, a period which found me struggling to maintain a simple process of self-realization through repeated mental viewings of my previous reports. The events that transpired both before and after the months of April and May are immaterial as far as I am concerned even if for the simple fact that the events (or non-events as they have been previously labeled by some) by no means caused anything that transpired during the months of April and May.

I am no fool. I know my place in the scheme of things even if that place is somewhere tucked away between the pages of a moldy apocalyptic book in some unkempt library of a suburban town that is both small and insignificant, a town that has ceased to grow in population as a result of the outdated information in their town hall meetings as well as the library where the moldy apocalyptic manuscript is located, harboring divine and not-so-divine symbology misshapen by archaic phraseology and whatever else you'd expect from such an ancient tome in an unimportant town.

If not for the fact that I harbor such ill will for all the ignorant members of that town council, I would replace the library's books with new editions of popular books, books that would tear open and dissect the headlines of today and tomorrow, books that would throw all embarrassing caution to the wind and wolves, and provide the population with entertainment and education with a most particular value. (But my ill will prevents me from doing such a deed. I am known to hold grudges and I am fine with that fact.)

My report will show that not only have I had patience enough for sainthood but I have also proven myself to be a reliable source of information not only about this hypothetical town and its council but also myself.

But this town council and the town it councils is, like I mentioned above, theoretical at best. My report will show that more often than not I have been the victim of self-sabotage and because of that, I have set up internal defenses which rival the gates of any given heaven.

When will my report be ready? It will be ready as soon as I make the appropriate corrections and I pass it along to my editors who, believe it or not, have enough faith in me to leave me alone for years on end. They allow me the time and space to finish my reports and for that, I am eternally grateful. They do not always approve of my actions (though, let's face it, who would approve of them after all that has transpired?) but they have always shown me the proper respect.

I'm losing my train of thought and soon the report will be lost in the mumbo-jumbo of other reports. That's happened before and when it does, it feels like my reports have come from Venus which is pretty silly when you think about it.

So with this, my report of the events, a report I will be sending to no one but myself, I SEEK TO JUSTIFY MY ACTIONS.

XIX. MEDITATION IS THE PRACTICE OF DEATH

Bunting looks over the footage from the previous day. It is crowd footage, establishing shots, research material. He enjoys the zooming in on unsuspecting people on the streets and in buildings. His attention is mostly on men but some women, too. The men are more interesting to him. They hold more secrets, more undercurrents of passionate energy. Bunting imagines their faces swelling with that energy, swelling until ready to burst, and then they do burst, and their dirty minds block out the sun.

He checks through the footage, all ten hours of it, in slow motion. Every second expands into four seconds and Bunting puts his nose to the television to be engulfed in the LCD light of a particular middle-aged man on the screen.

The man is normal looking. He is nondescript. He is quite boring.

But he is also impotent.

Bunting notices the man's slouching posture, his awkward movements that make his legs seem locked at the knees. Yes, the man is impotent.

Bunting pauses the tape and puts his cheek up to the screen. He enjoys the warmth, the fizzle of electricity.

He imagines the man naked, the pathetic shriveling of the genitals being preyed upon by the camera's eye, recorded and archived for posterity. It is a dead organ. It is a purposeless reminder of a lost regime, an archaic temple, cobwebbed hallways that are dry and full of echoes of limp spiders.

The thoughts of fellatio enter Bunting's mind but are quickly replaced by the idea of strapping explosives to the man's useless member and blowing it up in a fiery display of antiquated manhood.

Bunting realizes how melodramatic that would be.

True satisfaction comes from seduction that is strategic and quiet. It must be done with some level of grace and philosophical poignancy. It must be a result of meditation and submission.

He presses the PLAY button. He watches the man walk. He rewinds the tape and watches the man walk again.

He rewinds the tape and watches, watches, watches....

But the impotent man's actions do not change.

Bunting chants and rewinds, chants and rewinds. He meditates and submits, meditates and submits.

Soon there is nothing left but a camcorder haze in Bunting's eyes. A ghost in the shape of the impotent man floats in the air, twisting into electric submission. It falls at Bunting's feet like a translucent mass of spineless ectoplasm.

Bunting grabs the video camera, points it at a mirror, and presses RECORD.

XX. BELIEVE IN LODGES

You are not in a residential area. You are not safe. You are not where you thought you were. It is nighttime so everything is dark and silent.

You are in an industrial park. You are standing on the asphalt of a parking lot of a corporation named MONS GRAUPIUS, INC. You wonder what they make but the sign is too abstract and gives no indication as to the business they are in.

Your bowels start to loosen. That always happens when you are alone somewhere unfamiliar or when you are hiding. But are you hiding? You do not know. It is quite possible that you are hiding from someone (or something) but you would like to assume that's not the case. You do not feel like running or hiding. You do not want to have to defecate while running or hiding.

You walk through the parking lot into another. You look up at the sign for ATRAX LABS and assume they perform some sort of scientific service. You imagine mad scientists. You imagine bubbling test tubes and crazy laughter. You know that is ridiculous but you let your mind wander in that direction anyway. It is comforting mixing fantastical thoughts with mundane reality. It is as if you are dreaming when you are not.

You hear a car in the distance. Who is it? Security? Police? You quickly run in the other direction and find yourself standing in front of yet another business. You are shocked by the name because it sounds so familiar.

BUTTO BUTTO CORPORATION.

Why is it so familiar? You do not remember. You do not want to remember. You just want to get away from the sound of the car.

You duck into the doorway and stand with your back against the glass. You move your hand behind your back and check the door. Much to your surprise, it's open. The cleaning people must still be inside.

You do it.

You go inside.

You lock the deadbolt behind you.

You're inside the BUTTO BUTTO CORPORATION building. Now what?

The lights are on. Someone is in here with you. You assume it's the cleaning crew but what if you're wrong? What if it's the employees of BUTTO BUTTO? You could probably talk your way out of things with the cleaning people being that they probably don't speak much English anyway and are more likely to be understanding to your plight. You imagine the employees of BUTTO BUTTO will find your presence to be threatening and will surely call the police.

You must be quiet.

You walk down the hallway. You walk through a door that enters into another hallway, one with a carpeted floor and doors on the left and right sides. All of the doors are closed.

You walk down that hallway. You glance at the names on the doors. Some seem foreign but a few are familiar: Julie Antler, Barry Quir, Dixon Lambert.

You are tempted to try each door even though any of them could potentially lead to your being caught. Your bowels loosen again. Your mind goes back to your childhood when you used to play Hide and Seek. You remember defecating in a neighbor's side yard because you could not take the suspense. You had been hiding for ten minutes and it was killing you. You pulled down your pants and let it slide out of you like a snake. It was easier than you thought. You then changed your hiding spot so no one would find your mess.

You reach the end of the hall where there is a door to a stairwell. You quietly open that door. There is only one way to go: up. So you go up.

Up.

The light bulb in the stairwell is bright. It hurts your eyes. You squint and walk up the steps. You reach the entrance to the second floor and open the door to see an identical hallway as the one on the ground level. You walk down the hall and notice the only discernible difference: the names on the doors.

Here on the second floor there is no Julie Antler. Barry Quir does not have an office here. Dixon Lambert is nowhere to be found. For some reason this upsets you, makes you nervous, anxious. You remember reading a book called *A Brief History of Industrial Parks*. You don't remember when or where you read it but you know you did. The memory of that book has chosen to arise at this very moment even though it might have been years since you have read it. You suspect you might have read it in a dream and that no such book actually exists.

You stop at the end of the hall and read a sign that says OFFICE MANAGER in large, bold letters.

You think you hear something from inside the room and instead of walking away to elude detection, you put your ear to the door and listen.

You listen.

XXI. THREE-FOURTHS OF A MILE IN TWO SECONDS

"…isn't like you don't have dozens of them stashed away."

"That's not the point, Roy."

"Then what is the point?"

"Point is I don't feel comfortable handing one off to you especially considering what you plan to do with it."

"There's nothing wrong with my plans."

"Except that they're insane."

"Don't talk to me about insanity."

"Roy, as far as I'm concerned, this conversation is over."

"Can you at least think about it?"

"I already thought about it."

"No you didn't! I just asked you!"

"Will you calm down please?"

"I'm calm. I'm just asking you to think about it."

"Listen, Roy, even if I wanted to give one to you, I wouldn't be allowed to."

"That's only if you make record of it…which you know you don't have to."

"You want me to lie for you? Risk my job?"

"It's not much of a risk and you know it. Besides, you owe me."

"For what?"

"The whole Swissair thing."

"Are you seriously going to bring that up now? You've been holding onto that after all these years?"

"I haven't been holding onto anything. I totally forgot about it until recently. Now I'm just calling in a long overdue favor."

"Christ, Roy."

"You knew I was going to come calling eventually. Let's not pretend we do favors for nothing. It's give and take."

"Yeah, I know."

"So, I'm officially cashing this one in."

"Jesus Christ, Roy."

"Jesus Christ yourself. Now let's have it. It isn't like you don't have dozens of them stashed away."

"That's not the point, Roy."

"Then what is the point?"

"Point is I don't feel comfortable handing one off to you especially considering what you plan to do with it."

"There's nothing wrong with my plans."

"Except that they're insane."

"Don't talk to me about insanity."

XXII. SIDE TRACKING

Barry finds a VHS tape left by his wife. A note is attached that says, "Maybe this will help? Take a look at it. Maybe we can watch it tonight."

He puts the tape into the VCR and presses PLAY.

There are commercials first. Women on couches hold phones up to their ears, the wires wrapped around their wrists. They tell him to call in to confess his deepest desires, his most hidden fantasies which they will grant, of course, for a price. It will cost him $3.99 for the first minute and $1.99 for each additional minute. He's slightly tempted but only because the idea of calling and talking about sexual intercourse seems like such a foreign and disorienting idea, like holding a séance in a dream. He wonders what such an experience would be like.

Barry is worried that the woman would expect him to lead her into the fantasy which he knows he would not be able to do. He would not be able to start the proceedings, to lubricate the sexual tension. There would be minute after minute of awkward silence and each of those minutes would cost him money. Finally the woman on the other end of the phone would start rambling obscene mantras until Barry either hangs up or ejaculates. Both would be uncomfortable and embarrassing.

He shudders at the thought.

There are five commercials in all. Two feature stereotypical pornographic actresses of indecipherable age. Their facial features make them look in their late 30s but their make-up and the lighting make them appear much younger. The next commercial features an Asian woman in stereotypical (and slightly offensive)

Oriental attire. The fourth has an African-American woman in a business suit or rather what's left of it after she tore part of it off in lust as she awaits your call. The last commercial features an older woman with drooping, gargantuan breasts. She offers to teach young callers a few tricks. She knows you want to call. She knows Barry wants to call.

Barry does want to call.

He wonders what would happen if he did. The commercial itself looks as if it was a few years old. Would the phone number still work?

His curiosity (mostly a nonsexual one) is too much to resist and he picks up the phone to dial. He reads the number of the older woman with drooping, gargantuan breasts.

He dials.

XXIII. BLACK BONE LEY

"Thank you for calling, you young stud. We value your call. If you know your party's extension, please press it now. Otherwise stay on the line to speak to an operator......"

Barry presses nothing.

"If you know your party's extension, please. If you know your party's extension, please. If you know your party's extension, please. Otherwise stay on the line speak to a <static/white noise> bla...giraf.."

Barry still does not press a button.

"<static/whitenoise>   ...bla...giraf...bla...giraf...   To speak to the older woman with drooping, gargantuan breasts dial one thousand nine hundred and eighty. For a younger woman dial one thousand three hundred twenty three... or, please hang up and try <white noise>."

Barry does not make a move. He stays on the line and listens:

"Ger ger ger ger ger ger ger ger ger ger ger ger ger ger.." (ad nauseum)

XXIV. RESPONDED WITH SEIZURES

I am in my parents' house and it is primed for demolition.

It is one of those situations in which I do not really know what to feel. Yes, it is the house I lived in since birth to age nineteen. Yes, it is the house wherein most of my childhood memories were formed. I took my first steps in here. I babbled my first words in here. I played with my toys. I watched television. I ate dinner with my family. I was sent to my room for bad behavior.

All in this very house.

But it is still just a manmade structure of wood and other assorted building materials. It does not seem realistic to expect it to last forever or to bask in the glory of nostalgia. It was never a great house, never a strong house. Thunderstorms would often knock shingles off the roof and shake the walls so hard that as a child I would cower underneath my blankets, hugging my stuffed raccoon so tight as to strangle it to a heaven of inanimate objects.

So the house itself is not something I value. Of course I am grateful I had a place to go home to and people to take care of me there. Unlike millions of people in the world, I had a place to call home. I am not a lunatic who thinks living on the street would have been a better choice. I am thankful for that place, that human hive I called my home.

But what now? Both my parents are gone and their house, like all their possessions inside, is just a decomposing reminder of their finite importance in the scheme of things.

I am a little embarrassed to admit I am eagerly awaiting the demolition of the thing. I believe I will gain some satisfaction, some closure that will lead me to a more fulfilling remainder of my days for I will eventually be like the house: weak and unwanted. I will eventually be primed for demolition. I am a little embarrassed to admit that I am eagerly awaiting that appointment, too. I believe I will gain some satisfaction, some closure that will lead to a more fulfilling eternity or non-eternity.

The truth is I am looking forward to the actual destruction. I have only seen devastation and ruin on television. All of if had seemed so false or so quaint. All of the damage had been contained in one box, one screen, one moment of observation that could be, with a click of a button, changed to a moment of comedic nonsense or commercial seduction. Televised destruction is comfortable and controllable. But witnessing the demolition of my parents' house will be, without a doubt, my first real experience of monumental ruin.

And I'm looking forward to it.

To my neighbors, however, I imagine their only thoughts will be about the noise or the mess and eventually thoughts about what will be built on the property. Their perspective of the destruction is so different from mine as to almost make it an event in some parallel universe. What they see, I do not see. What I see, they cannot see.

I have chosen not to empty the house of all my parents' possessions. It would have taken days, most likely weeks, for me to painstakingly separate the garbage from the nostalgia and knowing myself, I would have given up halfway through anyway. Why waste the time?

Everything will go down with the house.

Everything will go down: the termite-infested wood and scarred sheetrock and wallpaper half-unglued and dusty knickknacks and Christmas ornaments and outdated medical books and garage sale toys and tattered magazines and stainless steel dinnerware and so on and so forth.

But I am not being completely truthful. There is one thing I will save from the destruction.

There is one of my grandfather's fishing poles in the basement. It is not an expensive one. It's not a fancy one. It's quite outdated and I would be surprised if it was still in working condition. But for some reason I cannot let that go down with the house. So I will save it. I will save it despite the fact that I have never gone fishing nor do I have any plans to.

I've never been much of a fisherman. I've never been much of anything, really. I haven't been anything but a son waiting for things to play out to a final resolution, to some final moment of closure.

So I'm in my parents' house and I'm waiting. Just waiting.

XXV. INVOCATION OF BATHINOTH NEWS AT 11

Dr. Corbelli looks over Tina's papers. He knows most of the answers are lies but that does not matter to him. He can and will go through with the procedure she seeks. After all, he had taken an oath, had he not? He is a good doctor, is he not?

He is with Tina in the examination room and has her discuss, in detail, her two penises. The patient is obviously uncomfortable and that makes Dr. Corbelli even more eager to delve into the procedure. A disturbed mind is a pliable mind and in a patient such as Tina, it is an invaluable tool for experimentation, for gnosis.

The doctor says, "I think we can help you."

"Yeah?" Tina's previously frowning mouth curls into something akin to a smile.

"Yes, but it will be a very complex and very expensive procedure." Dr. Corbelli gently puts down the file folder onto the counter and puts his hands together. "Obviously we want to help you but…there is a question of cost…since you don't have any insurance…"

Tina's chin falls to her chest. She cries.

The doctor touches her leg. "But there are arrangements we can make."

A look of horror appears on Tina's face.

Dr. Corbelli takes a step back. "Oh no! No, no, I did not mean that! The arrangements I speak of involve medical testing."

"Testing?"

"Yes, testing you can get paid for and use towards your procedure."

"I…I guess that will be okay."

"We can discuss the details later. First, I need to examine you. I must take many notes if we are to have a successful procedure."

Tina nods.

"Now, Tina, you need to undress and put on the gown."

"Right now?"

"Yes. Would you like me to leave the room?"

"Could you? If you don't mind?"

Dr. Corbelli nods his head. "Of course not. I will be back in a few minutes." He pats her on the knee. "Everything will be just fine. Fine, fine, fine."

XXVI. I AM N. CHILD OF N.

Jessica wakes up and walks to the window. She leans her forehead against the glass, looking at the insects below her.

She whispers words and wishes they were bombs.

Her father had talked about bombs once, hadn't he? Jessica remembers the conversation. He had been talking with her mother, talking about something someone had written about him in a book. Lies, he said. They were all lies.

Jessica takes a cassette recorder out of her purse and presses PLAY. She listens to her father's voice.

Someone once told me the hotel was primed for demolition. Like always, I had responded with skepticism.

I have never seen anything get destroyed. I have never seen anything ruined or in any state of decay. Perhaps I have lived a sheltered life but for all I know, every object, person, and idea is immune to any form of degeneration or decay. People, objects, and thoughts are frozen in time but allowed to move just enough to give the impression of progress, of an eventual movement towards some destiny far off in the future. It will be a future of sameness and of an unchanged maturity.

But, like I said, perhaps I have lived a sheltered life.

The hotel breaks into brazen gobs of drool that spill out into the streets and into the ocean, transforming everything into proud cocoons. Conspiratorial squid and bags of teeth and coins are removed from hidden pockets on the ocean floor and the teeth are strewn across the horizon like yellow ruins of an archaic nation.

The coins are eaten. The squid are blown up with bombs made of holy tomes. The ocean. It terrifies me.

Jessica presses STOP and puts the cassette recorder back into her purse.

She loves her father. She loves him despite his abrupt departure, despite his manic nights of working in the basement, working on things he could not tell her or her mother about. What was he doing? Was it anything illegal? Immoral? Was it the cause behind his jumping to his death from that hotel window?

Or was it the alleged experiments by the government that caused his death? Electrodes and drugs planting mushroom hysterics into her father's grey matter. Taborica II and Bromo-DragonFLY and 4-HO-MET (aka 44 HO-TEP). Some needles here, some caplets there, some machines that hum and make her father's brain tingle and smoke. Jessica remembers her father talking about the gongs and how they reverberate throughout their town.

Jessica leans her forehead against the window, looking at the people below her. She whispers words, delicate and loving words to her father and wishes they were suicide bombers falling into the earth's grey matter.

XXVII. CIRCULUS VITIOSUS DEUS

Automobiles, mailboxes, and storefronts explode. The situation is dangerous. Just yesterday a police officer's car was blown into bits, killing several young people who had the misfortune of being stopped for driving while under the influence of hallucinogens.

So today is really just like any other day. Perhaps it is a bit tenser, filled with anxiety for all those who venture out into the labyrinthine city but there is still hope in the perpetual death ethics of all the new society cults.

The skyscrapers sway slightly in the wind. If you look closely, you can see them sway and it is truly frightening. Any minute they could lean just a little too much and bend over like fingers ready to crush.

What will fall next? I imagine it will be the person next to you. They will come crashing down in a last emotional effort to prove the dominance of their own private Moloch.

But the workday will go on. Most people will adapt to the change. They will show great resolve. They are hard-working people despite their dangerously high consumption of fluoride in the form of pale pills prescribed for their nervousness.

You might want to think about getting undressed. The videographers will be here shortly. I assume you've read the script.

*

Three hundred women use one large computer to enter data. They double and triple check each other's work. They print out copies of the data and place them in filing cabinets. They lock the filing cabinets and enter more data into the computer.

Each tap of the keyboard and click of the mouse brings a distinct code, an aural trigger that is vital to the women's work day. The clicks and clattering form music and force the women to tap along with their high-heeled feet. The sound of the high heels creates a din that shakes the foundation of the building, making the skyscraper sway dangerously with their incantations.

The din translates into mantras that sprout digitalized incarnations of their hard work, the sweat of their brows, their underarms, and their grey matter.

They continue to type.

Click-clack.

They type.

Click-clack.

As dusk approaches, the women stand up at their desks and stretch, revealing the sweat stains under their arms. They form an orderly line, wave at the security cameras, and make their way out the doors.

It's the end of their work day.

XXVIII. PERPETUAL FREEDOM

And the video store harbors drugged diamond boxes… and that Middle Eastern filmmaker behind the building pays no mind. He films the imaginary killer.

Father. Father. Father.

The filmmaker reads from the book…..

……effects of AIDS on homosexual men in the early 1980s and that was about the time he had worked for the government.

Could it be that some of his computer work contributed to those studies?

Out of his apartment building walks Tim Osman Spears who lights a cigarette and stands on the sidewalk, blowing smoke into spirals and blocks, humming and belching and singing songs within his skull to dispel the rumors he is telling himself. He looks at the sign hanging in a storefront. It says: WELCOME TO POMPEII!

He thinks he is in danger (he is probably right) but he tries to persuade himself to look beyond all tell-tale signs and have faith in the –

What?

Tim does not know.

Or maybe he forgets. He doesn't know which.

He thinks he's being filmed. He waves to all four corners of the earth. He thinks: I am the filmmaker and I am the film. I am the chemist and I am the chemical. I am the bomb maker and I am the bomb.

Tim Spears puts his cigarette to his face, feels the heat, and tries to imagine a small bomb exploding in his cheek.

He acknowledges his paranoia. He wants to walk around and observe, to film others, to film himself. It will be a way of being a part of society *without actually taking part in society.*

He tries to talk himself out of it but there is a delay in his speech. There is a delay in his thinking. He wonders and waits, wonders and waits. Opens his mouth to speak and waits and waits. Then the words come out, they spill out from his lips, from his tongue and teeth and shatters the air with incantations.

Who am I? What have I done?

These words split the cigarette smoke into intangible sigils:

I am just a producer of pornographic commercials. That's all I am, all I'll be remembered for or forgotten for or whatever. Hire some girls, give them some mushrooms, hand them a phone that does not work, tell them to talk to the camera, tell them they are beautiful, tell them they will be stars, they are important or if that doesn't work, tell them it's just a job, of course they're better than this but they need the money after all, just pretend. I write them a check and hope it doesn't bounce. I sit in the studio alone with the lights off, sitting on the couch the women have been sitting on. I try to inhale their scent, try to recapture that intimate aspect of those faceless women. But there's nothing. I smell only leather and disinfectant and my own cheap cologne and armpit smell but I really want to smell their sweat and their musk and their shampoo and every- thing else that makes them better than me.

Maybe I don't want to come back to this. Maybe some bombs aren't meant to detonate.

Oh, don't say that kind of thing, Tim. Let's go to a video store and rent some of your classics. It'll take your mind off things.

I don't want to. It's always too difficult to make a decision.

Every decision is difficult.

But everything is more difficult for me.

Don't be so melodramatic. You're a grown man. Shit or get off the pot. Do what you want to do or don't do anything at all. Do whatever you want, when you want.

So what now?

What do you think? We do something we've never done before, something that will give us meaning, closure….something that will connect the alpha and the omega so you can be calm again. You know, something that will be meaningful but banal. It's all about closure, about reconciliation of the soul.

So what are we going to do?

We're going to go fishing.

THE
GOG AND MAGOG BUSINESS

Sooner or later, everything turns into television.
 - J.G. Ballard

Dedicated
to
Rabbi Moshe ben Nahman
and
Dr. A. Silverman

Every man has inside himself a parasitic being who is acting not at all to his advantage
-William S. Burroughs

I. GINNAT EGOZ

He says, "We're all in danger, you know."

I shrug him off, ignore him as usual, and continue with our rounds. I check each room, each patient, and each chart.

"Everything's fine," I say to him.

"Someone's thinking about us," he says. "Right now someone is thinking about doing us in. Killing us. Get it?"

I shrug and hand him a chart for him to sign. "Sure, I get it."

He grabs the chart but doesn't sign. He stares down the hall. "You ever hear the rumors about those guys who work the nightshift downstairs?"

"Can you just sign the chart?"

"Have you?"

"No. Now can you just sign it?"

"Come on, have you heard?" he says, signing the chart slowly.

The thing is: yes, I have heard the rumors but I have no desire to talk about it with him. There are plenty of rumors here and rarely do any of them turn out to be true.

"Yeah, I heard them," I say. I make sure I am showing no enthusiasm whatsoever.

"So?" he says. "What do you think?"

"What do I think about what?"

"Do you think it's true?"

"Jesus, I don't know. Does it really matter?" I say, walking faster down the hall, trying to quicken our pace so that maybe, just maybe, we'd get done with our rounds by a decent hour.

"You're not even curious," he says. He doesn't seem to care about the pace I'm trying to set. In fact, it appears that he's walking even slower now.

"Will you come on already? I want to get this done soon."

"We'll be done when we're done," he says. "So what do you think about the nightshift guys?"

I don't answer him. I go to the next room, check the patient, check the chart, sign my name to the chart, and then forge his name as well. He doesn't notice. I didn't think he would.

He flicks me on the back. "You want to check it out after we're done?"

"Check what out?"

The nightshift guys. See what they're up to."

"No, I really don't."

"Come on. It's no big deal."

"I know it's not. That's why I'm saying no."

We finish the rest of the rounds in silence. I am doing most of the work but I'm used to it. He was always thinking about one rumor or another, anything to keep him away from the work at hand. What does that mean for me? That means I have to pick up his slack. But like I said, I'm used to it.

It's the end of our shifts.

He finally speaks. "You sure?"

I look him in the eyes and say, "I'm sure. Good night."

I walk away and can hear him groan my name.

II. KAVANNAH WAVES

I guess there is something fairly sweet about the taste and something fairly foreboding about the texture. We aren't sure what exactly we are eating but we're stuffing it into our mouths nonetheless. Whenever there is food left in the break room, you can be damn sure people are going to eat it.

Someone taps me on the shoulder. It's the new guy. He's eager to earn my respect and I like that. I think my respect is worth earning. I nod to the new guy. He nods back.

He says, "So who brought this stuff in?"

"Don't know," I say, putting more of the food into my mouth.

"It's good."

"Yeah," I say. I want him to get away from me. I want him to shut his mouth and walk away. I can't tell him to do so because that would be unprofessional. Even I, someone who tends to shrug off professionalism, am reluctant to be so overt in my reaction.

"Hey, when you get a chance, there's something I want to show you."

When I get a chance? What does that mean? He's giving me no choice but to seek him out sometime during the day and I don't want to do that. In fact, I am contemplating leaving work early simply to avoid it. I could complain of stomach trouble and then just go home.

"Okay," I say. I glance down at the food, see that it's almost gone, and then quickly walk away. I hope he doesn't follow. I hope he takes the hint. He does. That's good.

On the way to my desk, I look out the window. There is something wrong outside. I'm not the most observant of people. That's the truth. There have been plenty of times when I have "lost" something only to find out it was right in front of my face the entire time. I'm not a fool, though. I'm just generally uninterested in the world around me. That's not an attempt to sound intellectually deep especially since what's usually occupying my mind is quite banal anyway.

I am staring out the window and I'm not blinking. I am just staring at what's out there and realizing that something is out of place. There is movement where there shouldn't be movement.

Something is quite wrong.

Someone is behind me now. It's the new guy but fortunately he doesn't say a word to me. He is staring out the window.

Everyone is staring out the window.

III. HONEY FROM ROCKS

The structures are just shapes against the sky. They do not represent anything except shapes. Their significance does not extend beyond being simple structures in the midst of other structures.

Jacob recites these words and finishes his sketch.

Everything is perfect. His drawing of the structures represents more than the structures themselves which was Jacob's intention when he began the project.

There are people around him but he does not notice. They are simply small breezes against his skin. They are small pockets of noise against his ears. They are mechanisms of distraction but he will not be distracted.

He holds the sketch up to the sky and wonders what it would take to build those structures in the sky so they floated with the clouds. What a silly idea! He quickly dismisses it. These structures aren't meant to float. They are meant to be drawn and redrawn, built and rebuilt, destroyed and destroyed and destroyed.

Jacob rips the picture out of the sketchbook and hands it to a young man in a suit. The young man takes the paper, looks at the drawing, and walks away with it. Over his shoulder, the young man says, "That plane's flying pretty low, isn't it?"

Jacob looks up into the sky but sees no plane.

A young woman in a business skirt bumps into him and says, "Pardon."

"Excuse me," Jacob says. He wants to quickly draw another sketch to hand to the young woman.

She gives Jacob a puzzled look. "You hear that?"

"What?"

"That roar."

"What roar?" Jacob hears nothing. No, he does hear something. He hears the crumpling of paper. He sees the young man in the suit crumpling up his drawing and throwing it into a trash bin.

Jacob wants to run to the bin and retrieve his sketch. It is not something that should be discarded like mere trash.

He doesn't run. He looks back at the woman but she is already on her way.

Jacob closes his eyes and hugs his sketchbook to his chest. Yes, he hears the roaring now. He peeks through his eyelids and looks at the sky. Yes, there is something there, something that is flying too low.

He shuts his eyes tight and stares into the darkness.

"Watch out!" Jacob says. He screams it into the darkness. He screams it at the young man who had thrown his drawing away. He screams it at the young woman who had bumped into him. He screams it at everyone and everything.

He hears the crash. He feels the heat.

Jacob opens his eyes but sees only darkness.

IV. AYN-SOF DREAMS OF SOLAR LODGES

Sometimes I fall asleep to the sound of ominous spheres rolling down the hallway outside my door. Sometimes I awake to the sound of spherical doom opening and closing doors in the hallway outside. Sometimes I sit and listen to the soft babbling of my empty room as it smears interrupted silence on the surface of my gloom.

But more often than not I pinch the skin between my thumb and index finger until the pain pushes me into blackness for I do not want to hear anything but my dry skin cracking. That is what brings me those dreams of hiding in an industrial park.

I hide in doorways and corridors and janitor's closets and under desks and in bathroom stalls and closets filled with medication. I hide and feel my bowels nervously rumble. In my dreams, I am never found.

Never mind that. My dreams are not important. No one's dreams are important. All dreams are bastard offspring of babbling brains. They try to escape to the dusty corners of the ceiling where cobwebs catch them, ingest them, and wrap them in plastic to sell in five-and-dime shops where frugal housewives buy them for their children so the little pests won't cry. I should know. My mother took me to five-and-dime shops when I was a child. More times than not I would come out holding a cheaply made action figure or toy robot.

So it is Friday afternoon and Tim asks me if I want to drive up to his college with him. "It'll be fun," he says. "We'll just stay in the library and read."

"Why do you need me for that?" I ask.

"I like company when I read," he says. "Besides, we won't have a lot of distractions there and I know you wanted to finish up your little project."

"Okay."

And so I drive up to the college with him. As soon as we approach the campus I know I have made a mistake. It has been years since I have stepped foot anywhere near that place and I now remember why that is so. The college seems to suck all the psychic fluid from me until there is nothing left but a crude construction of bones topped with a sentient prune inside a pale cranium.

"Something wrong?" Tim asks. "You look like shit."

"Nothing's wrong. I'm just…" I say but I never finish the sentence. Instead, I open the door to the library and start up the flight of stairs that will bring me to the third floor.

"Why do you want to go to the third floor?" Tim asks.

"I don't know. Why not?"

"I don't know."

We find a table in the corner and sit down. I set my bag down on a chair and go off looking for a book. Tim has already picked one up on the way. It is a seemingly random choice but knowing Tim, it might have been planned weeks in advance. I don't see the title but I know it is something about antler jelly.

I leave him at the table and walk to the far corner of the room. The books there are dusty and look untouched. It is as if college students don't read anymore. I expect the books to be mere props. I run my fingers along the spines, pushing them inward to feel the weight of them, just to make sure they are real.

After a few minutes of perusing I find a book that interests me.

I sit down on the floor and start to read. Sitting next to Tim isn't something I really want to do. He moves his lips while he reads. He also has mild body odor like cheese. Besides, my little project requires unconventional reading environments and the library floor seems to fit that description.

What is my project? It's…

Tim touches me on the shoulder. "What the hell are you doing?"

"I'm reading," I say. A sound on the other side of the shelf makes us both turn our heads. It is the sound of a heavy sphere rolling through sludge. Then: doors open and close followed by wordy dreams being sucked through brown cotton until they scrape the dull paint on my walls and form bulbous pyramids of black glue.

"Let's go," I say. "I'm going to check this book out."

"You can't."

"Why not?"

"They're closing the library at the end of the semester and they want all the books in. You can only read them in here or…"

"Or what?" I ask.

"Or you can steal them."

"I have no problem with that."

Tim nods. "Didn't think you would."

We walk quickly down the aisle, turn right, and go down the stairs. Dizziness sets in. I see a janitor mopping a floor. A librarian is leading a nervous young student up the stairs. A dog barks in the distance.

I duck into a corner and open the back of the book where they keep the security sensor. After an impromptu surgery with my ballpoint pen, the sensor is out and I am free to adopt the book as my own.

When we go outside I notice how cold it has become. Normally I don't notice things like the weather but this time the temperature slaps me in the face. Tim grabs my arm and leads me to the next building. "In here," he says.

"Why?"

"I gotta show you something."

I stand in front of the door to the new building and look at my reflection in the glass doors. The library is no longer behind me. It is an industrial park filled with 18-wheelers hauling merchandise, pallets of plastic-wrapped boxes, and stocky, sweaty workers operating worn-out forklifts.

Tim opens the door for me and I walk inside.

In front of me is a vending machine offering candy bars and potato chips. I dig in my pocket because I usually keep a little bit of change on me. This time, however, I am broke. "Got some quarters?" I ask Tim.

"Nope."

"Dollar bills?"

"Nope."

"Well then…" I say, disappointed but understanding. Tim is usually broke. I don't even know why I had expected him to have any money.

We walk down a hallway that is lined with brick walls and trophy cases. Occasionally there is a framed picture of some obscure aspect of biology or architecture.

"What building are we in?" I ask.

"Building Three."

"No, I meant, like…" I start but stop when we approach some doors.

The doors open revealing an extremely large but empty elevator. There is a sound like someone punching a bag of rice. I used to eat a lot of rice when I was in college. White rice with processed American cheese melted on top. I had probably eaten that for five out of seven dinners each week. The other times I ate a few bowls of some generic cereal. It was never extravagant but it's all I was able to afford and to be honest, it's all I really wanted to eat.

We step into the elevator and Tim presses the button for the third floor.

"Where are we going?" I ask.

"I have to drop something off."

"Where?"

"Third floor."

"No, I meant, like…" The elevator starts and then stops quickly. I almost fall over. Now I notice my bladder is full.

"There a bathroom on the third floor?"

"Probably," Tim says. "Yes, I'm pretty sure there definitely is."

The doors open and we step out into a bright hallway that does not look like a college. If I knew any better I would have to say it belongs in some sort of office building in an industrial park.

"Where are we going?" I say.

"Down here," Tim says, leading me down the hallway and then down another corridor to the right. This hallway is darker than the first and smells like cheese being cooked in a microwave.

"What's that sound?" I say. It is like a tin sphere being attacked with spoons.

"Dunno," Tim says. "I've never been here before."

"Where? The third floor?"

"No."

"This building?"

"No, this college."

"What do you mean?"

"I've never been here before."

We reach the end of the hall. The burning cheese smell is stronger and so is the sound of sphere versus spoons.

The door is barely visible on the brick wall as if drawn in chalk. But indeed it is a real door because Tim opens it with a slight push to the center.

"Thanks for coming with me," Tim says.

"No problem," I say.

We walk into my bedroom and I sit in front of my bookshelf. I randomly grab a book and set it down in front of me. Tim also grabs a book but throws it on my bed.

"Your books smell old," he says.

"That's a weird thing to say."

"But it's true."

I nod, open my book, and start reading something about licorice and conspiracies. Some man named Bayley had come up with some crazy ideas about hooded men in helicopters and the soft stars they conspire against.

Tim sits on the edge of my bed. "You tired?"

"Not yet."

"I'm going to use the bathroom," Tim says, getting up from the bed. He walks out the door and slams it shut.

My eyes blink through the book on my lap. Now the sounds come.

The toilet flushes and spheres spiral down the staircase and onto the wooden floors. I hear them roll into the furniture, into the walls, into the silence like manic round vacuums.

Tim slams the bathroom door, opens it, and slams it harder. It opens once again. His footsteps echo in my bathtub. The faucet turns on. Water splashes on his shoes. I hear his shoelaces become limp with moisture.

"What are you doing in there?" I shout. No answer. "Don't make a mess!"

The bathroom door slams shut. The sound of it combines with the clunking of the spheres as they make their way back up the stairs.

There was a time years ago when the stairs were covered in toys causing my father to trip and break his neck. He had died instantly. But now the spheres are the only toys haunting the steps.

A scream breaks through my bedroom door. It takes me longer to get up off the floor than I expect. I feel old and rusty like an unused bicycle. I throw open the door and look into the hallway. At the bottom of the steps Tim is sprawled out like an octopus.

He has fallen down the stairs.

I know at this moment my gloom will become legendary.

All around me the wallpaper falls down in strips: tongues with stale glue and unwanted paint calling me into the bathroom where I'll find the black sun deep within the drain.

I turn the water on to flush it out while behind me the spheres shuffle into an obscure formation I've never seen before.

The water refuses to go down the drain and stays on the outskirts of the sink, refusing to be burned beneath my sink. The water's flesh crawls around the faucet and onto my hand.

I spit fire, burning my fingers into loops. They fall down the drain, unwilling to bow to the sun in fear.

I think of Tim.

My gloom turns to soft babbling hope.

I run out of the bathroom and down the stairs, dodging imaginary toys and hysterical strips of fatherly wallpaper. Tim's body has turned more grotesque. It resembles chewing gum stretched over a bundle of broken sticks.

"Get up," I say. "Get up."

He twitches but does not get up.

I walk back upstairs and into my room. I take the elevator back to the first floor and walk outside back to the library. The stairs to the third floor are covered in hollow trinkets that trip me up at every opportunity. I make it to the top, though.

It takes me only a minute to find the book: *A Brief History of Industrial Parks* by Julie Antler.

I sit down on the floor between the stacks of books, adjusting my pants so I'd be most comfortable. The florescent lights above me flicker and buzz in code.

I start to read. The pages smell like old age and doom. Words upon words slip through the haze of my most recent memories. Antler briefly explains the history of the pallet.

Paper cuts spread across my hands like rivers on maps. My knuckles are broken apart like five-and-dime toys. I pinch the skin between my thumb and index finger.

It doesn't take me long to fall asleep to the sound of gloomy spheres and soft babbling of unread books.

V. ATZMUS OHR EIN SOF LIFNEI HATZIMTZUM

It goes without saying that I should probably explain the events leading up to my current situation. This situation I'm in is dire, yes, but I've pretty much accepted my fate or accepted it as much as you'd expect any person to under the circumstances.

Four weeks ago I received a call from our recruitment office in Manhattan. Someone had sent an anonymous package which contained five-hundred photocopied pages of a document we had thought was lost to history. Not only did we think it was lost but we wanted it lost.

Someone had gone to the trouble of copying all of those pages and sending it to our recruitment office, knowing full well that word would get to me and that I would take the first flight to NYC in order to investigate. At the time, I did not know who that someone was but in hindsight, there shouldn't even have been a question. There should have never been a mystery.

Our ignorance led me to where I am right now: writing a document while I am huddled in a homeless shelter. Me, a person who had everything anyone could ask for. I am wrapped in a flea infested blanket. I feel them biting. There may be other small insects on the blanket as well. There are surely microscopic germs on this blanket, too. I think I can hear them mumble and breed. I am sure they are planning their own little coup. However, if I am to be honest, perhaps I am the one who has taken over their territory, their dominion, and therefore they would have every right to overthrow my presence. I am surely a god to those pitiful yet powerful germs.

If there is one thing I need you to keep in mind while you read my documentation is this: the possibility of ascent is all the time.

So when the recruitment office received the package, they contacted me and I took the next flight to NYC despite my extreme fear of flying. Previously I had only traveled to the east coast via train or bus. However, this incident in question was something that needed to be taken care of as quickly as possible and so I boarded a plane with a head full of anti-anxiety medication.

When I reached NYC, I was a foggy mess. That was okay, though. With the help of some prescription head-clearers, I got focused and took a cab to the recruitment office. When I got there, all I saw was the swirling lights of law enforcement. That was not a good sign. Then I saw the ambulances and the fire trucks.

The recruitment center (consisting of five floors in a 25 story building) was no more. Someone had piloted a small passenger plane into the fourth and fifth floors. The place was on fire. The back part of the plane (I don't know the technical term) was sticking out and I remember that it reminded me of the tail of a shrimp.

In the crowd gathering outside the building, I spotted Peter. The cab let me out and I slowly slid beside him. "Hey," I said.

"Oh, you're here."

"Yeah, Peter, I'm here. What the hell happened?"

"What do you think?"

"Yeah, I know, I mean, what happened to the...package...?"

Peter shrugged. "The last I saw of it, Tim had it. Then the plane hit, the police and fire trucks showed up, and that was that. We all ran out. Don't know where Tim went, though. I'm worried about him."

"I'm worried about the package."

Peter gave me that look. You know. The "you're heartless" look. But I was used to it. When you are in the higher echelons of an organization, you tend to prioritize very objectively. Don't get me wrong: I've always liked Tim and I think he's a strong member of the group. However, the contents of the package were much more important in the long run.

That's when I spotted the guy on the bicycle. He was watching the fiery building with the rest of the crowd but he kept looking back at Peter and me. The guy had a long neck and a face covered in birth marks. He looked like a giraffe.

I didn't really care about the fact that the guy was looking at us but then I saw what was under his arms. It looked like thick envelope full of paper.

"Hey Peter."

"Yeah?"

"Look at that guy over there on the bicycle. Is that the package?"

"Holy shit."

"So that's it?"

"Yeah. Holy shit," Peter said. He started bouncing up and down on the heels of his feet. "What are we going to do?"

"I'm going to make my way over there."

"What do I do?"

"Just stay here."

So I made my way over to the giraffe on the bicycle and that's how I ended up here. That was four weeks ago.

VI. DRUNK IN THE HOUSE OF THE ENEMY

"Tell us another one, Barry," she says.

"I don't have another one."

"Oh, come on….you always have jokes!"

Barry puts down his drink on the coffee table and leans back on the couch. He grabs a cigarette from his pocket and lights it. "Okay, then…"

Three Middle Eastern men walk into a bar. The first man orders a cola and the bartender gives him a look of pity. The second man orders a light beer and the bartender gives him a look of shame. The third man orders nothing but instead he whispers something into the bartender's ear.

The bartender stands silent for a moment, nods his head, shakes his head, and then falls to the floor in tears.

The first man yells about his cola. The second man yells about his light beer. The third man whispers in the ear of the second man.

The second man listens and then sits silently for a moment. He nods his head, shakes his head, and then falls to the floor in weepy gasps.

The first man is still yelling about his cola.

Then suddenly there is an explosion.

Debris, flames, and smoke are everywhere.

The first man coughs, yells about his cola, coughs some more, and then drops dead right there on the barroom floor.

A few minutes later, three firefighters come in to put out the flames that have, by that time, decimated the bar.

The first firefighter looks at the flames and says, "I'm not too sure about this."

The second firefighter looks at the first firefighter and says, "You got to be kidding me."

The third firefighter looks at the flaming mountain of liquor and says, "Anyone want to buy me a drink?"

Then suddenly there is an explosion.

Three Middle Eastern men walk into the fire. The flames enrapture them like angel wings. They are lifted up into the air by the furious smoke of destructive djinn which is ironic since djinn usually aren't associated with smoke. The men's voices carried through the wind and circled the town in what one resident later described as a cacophony of syrupy chanting.

The owner of the bar, who was fortunately not present at the time of the explosions, would later rebuild her business using her late husband's life insurance money. Of course, the bar would never quite be the same. No matter what she did, she could never get rid of the smell of poppies and jet fuel.

VII. AND IN THOSE DAYS THE REAPERS SHALL NOT GROW WEARY

You lurk on the threshold.

Whoever invited you here must have made a mistake. Certainly you do not belong here. Certainly you cannot simply walk through the doorway and into the building without feeling like this is all just a mistake.

Are you coming in? Are you just going to stand there?

There you go. Good job. Walk right in and expect things to work out. If it is just a mistake, I'm sure it can be resolved rather simply.

You are used to things working out to your advantage. You are used to things going well, going according to plan. Except for this. You were invited here and you have no idea why. It is an unexpected turn of events and that is why you are still lurking, standing meekly in the foyer.

You have been invited and it would be rude not to follow through. You have gotten this far. You must go through with it.

You take a few steps forward. Good. You take a few more and you get to the entrance of a hallway.

Now what?

You will go down that hallway, you know. You will go down that hallway and find a door that is unlocked. It does not matter which door, of course, since the invitation did not specify.

You go down the hallway, still hesitant but making progress nonetheless.

You notice that you are in a rather small hallway for such a large building. Was it intentional on the part of the architect? You do not know much about architecture but surely something is wrong with the hallway. Surely something is wrong with feeling so trapped in a building so large.

You find a door that is unlocked and you walk inside. You are now not so apprehensive. You do not lurk on the threshold of this room. Despite the pitch darkness you walk right inside.

The room is warmer than the hallway. You are sweating. You take off your shirt.

A light flickers in the corner of the room. You hear the sound of a computer humming. You hear typing. You hear muttered curses.

You ask if anyone is in the room.

No one answers you.

You ask again.

The typing stops. The light flickers out. You no longer hear the hum of the computer.

You are ushered out of the room by two frail but invisible hands.

You are back in the hallway but now it is filled with people. The size of the crowd is making you nervous. What are you going to do? Where are you going to go? You certainly cannot decline the invitation at this late an hour.

Someone bumps into you. They pardon themselves and move on. Everyone is going into one doorway and then out another. The only room they do not go near is the dark one you were ushered out of.

You are standing in the middle of a crowd of people you do not know in a building you are not familiar with in a city you are a stranger to. You decide that no invitation is strong enough to compel you to stay here in this whirlpool of confusion.

You walk back to the foyer and go outside. The sidewalk is not much better. There are people here, too. They all ignore you despite their insistence on knocking into you.

You hear the hum of the city. It is all machine and voices and beeps and honks and roars and screeches and every sound in the entire universe coalescing into an oppressive din. You have had enough.

You will no longer respond to invitations. You will not be a slave to social obligations.

You look at the city, spin around to see it in a panoramic view and decide that you would much rather see a cornfield or a farm.

Someone bumps into you and you fall to your knees. You put your forehead to the cement and start to mumble an incoherent prayer.

You lurk on the threshold of a doorway no one else can see.

VIII. RISING MOMENT OF CREATION

Someone once told me my body was primed for death.

Like always, I had responded with skepticism.

I have never seen anything get destroyed. I have never seen anything ruined or in any state of decay. Perhaps I have lived a sheltered life but for all I know, every object, person, and idea is immune to any form of degeneration or decay. People, objects, and thoughts are frozen in time but allowed to move just enough to give the impression of progress, of an eventual movement towards some destiny far off in the future. It will be a future of sameness and of an unchanged maturity.

But, like I said, perhaps I have lived a sheltered life.

When I arrive at the hotel, I find out that my room is on the top floor for which I am a little disappointed. I have a view of the ocean and I hate the ocean. I would much rather look out at the city with all its buildings puffing smoke, noise, and artificial light. Yes, there are too many people in the city, too many busy people who live to work and work to live. But they are a part of me, just like me. The ocean provides a horrifying blank slate for my thoughts whereas the urban landscape provides a reminder of the natural state of things, at the beautiful chaos that gives life to the very soul of a human being.

Upon entering the hotel room, I see that the housekeeper must have spent a good amount of time getting it ready. Everything is immaculate, even the television remote control which, from what I have heard, should be the filthiest thing in the room.

I sit on the bed, exhausted from the trip but not exhausted enough to lie down and nap. Sleep would be needed eventually but not yet. Things have to be done before I can give myself the luxury of dreaming. The dreams that I have been having were ones I really do not want to experience. They are dreams of space shuttles with no set course. They are of moons that are simply not right. They are dreams of documents I can never find no matter how long I look for them. They are hidden in the craters of the moons of my dreams. They are dusty, futuristic things. They are torn from supermarket tabloids full of death and impotence. They are the rising tide of disappointment on a universal scale.

The windows appear freshly washed. It is as if there is no glass separating me from the outside. I stand up and walk over to check for sure that there is something preventing me from falling out of the building. I put my hand out and touch the warm smoothness of the glass. I am worried its temperature will soon rise to the point of melting. I almost want to be burned by fiery glass. I almost want to fall out of the window.

I pull my hand away for it is like touching a warm corpse.

I stay put, looking out and watching the dark green sea as it ripples and pulsates. It is calling me from its infernal depths. I think it is safe to say now that the ocean had claimed my father and I cannot look at it without feeling some sort of duty to avenge his death. It is a silly thought, yes, since we all know the ocean is not a living, breathing thing. It is simply a monstrous force, the largest monstrous force on the planet and I am impotent against it.

After staring into its surface for a few minutes, hoping to see my father's arm rise up from the water, I go back to the bed and turn the television on with the freshly cleaned remote control.

Television provides me with life outside of my thoughts. But maybe I just like the noise. It produces sounds I don't have to take part in, voices I don't have to respond to. It is a way of being a part of society *without actually taking part in society.*

Therefore I have little need of real friends or family. Instead, I let the television programs act as the outside chaos that would otherwise engulf my senses and emotional stability. Television broadcasts never decay. They are, in a way, eternal.

I never follow any particular program, though. I don't make any effort to have the television on at any particular time. I let my whim dictate my interactions with the shows. The randomness of my viewing exposes me to a myriad number of life experiences. I never know what the day will bring.

This particular hotel room television is ancient. I am sure one of the dust-covered speakers is blown out because the noise sounds lopsided and muffled which makes everything that comes out of it resemble slow ocean waves. I am lulled into a state of anxiety. The television noise is the roar of the terrible waves. I await the rising up of a televised leviathan from the depths of the transmission. I am prepared to tear its belly open to retrieve my father.

It is during this state of anxiety that my body starts to collapse.

But it is also the hotel that is collapsing. It is a simultaneous demolition.

One would think such an event would be frightening and disorienting but I find it a relief, something akin to an orgasm. Finally, I will see what there is to see. Finally, I will gain all the knowledge there is to gain. I am no longer impotent.

There is a rumbling below me and I feel the bed drop out from under me and I am falling, the ceiling following me down along with the television. My stomach twists and my bowels churn, loosen, and are emptied into the air. My head is pounding with fever.

It is a dreamlike freefall. It cocoons my body in dust and noise. Every solid object turns to brown mist and I am engulfed in a noisy removal from the spider web of my existence.

I should have known this would happen. Someone once told me that everything everywhere was primed for demolition. But like always, I had responded with skepticism.

IX. TOMORROW WE WERE ALL ALIVE, WELL

The two groups are readying along the perimeter. They are disguised, as is to be expected, and they are overloaded with gear they may not even need.

I'm just an observer, you understand, and I am not in any position to take any action whatsoever. Therefore, I should not and will not be held accountable for whatever events transpire during my observation.

Someone puts the fan on and fills the bottles up with water. Another person records something in a thick notebook. A third person starts to dig a hole and we make eye contact. I don't do anything. I don't nod. I don't smile. I don't even blink. I am only an observer and even though I know that my very presence here will affect their actions, I am trying my best to minimize my influence.

I do have a camera, yes. I am documenting the events, yes. It does not matter what kind of camera I have just as long as I am documenting the events. For years I have studied how to do the best possible job with the worst possible equipment so the mechanisms I use for documentation do not matter as much as who is doing the documenting (which, in this case, is me).

The two groups are working as they should be and I believe all of the members have forgotten I am here. Even the one who has made eye contact with me is busy with his task. Again, I am the observer and I wish to not affect the observed.

There is more to it than that, however. Truthfully, I do not wish to become involved. I have not opinion on the matter whatsoever. If both groups stopped what they were doing and approached me, I would just stay put and continue with my camerawork. If they ask (or eventually, interrogate me) about my views on their work, I will assure them with a clear conscience that I hold no opinion on the issue nor do I foresee myself having one in the future. Whether or not they would believe me, well, that's a different story.

Two members of the first group walk up to the truck that has been repainted recently. In black cursive script the words *Mons Graupius Moving* have been painted on the sides. Under the words were pictures of crudely drawn smiley faces.

I zoom in on the truck and then on the faces of the members who start unloading boxes, crates, and garbage bags. I zoom out and follow the action as it moves to one of the office doors.

Entering the actual offices will be the most challenging part of this whole ordeal. I wouldn't go so far as to say I'm afraid, mind you, but I feel a bit of trepidation in stepping foot into that place, the hallowed ground of my predecessors. Those men and women who have done all of this before, they have accomplished so much more than I will ever hope to achieve. They have written books (fifty-one at last count) and submitted report after report on every possible aspect of this entire thing.

At times I feel like a simple cameraman despite the fact that I am so much more. Right now, though, I am only a keen observer and I am distracting myself with these comparisons and doubts.

I zoom in through the glass door.

I zoom in on a payphone.

I zoom in on a water fountain.

I zoom in on a man's face.

I zoom in on his mouth.

I zoom in on the pills in his mouth.

I zoom in on his throat as he swallows.

I can see the pills as they make their way down. I can see them enter his stomach and dissolve.

I zoom out.

I zoom in on the man's face and hold the shot as his mouth opens and he mouths some words. I cannot hear him through the glass doors but I can only imagine what he is saying.

"….simply any place over which I utter your names…."

"You must dip your pen in your black ink and write your name upon my tongue…."

"At the core of the city, the fungal magnificence of the building enthralls all who circle it…"

I nod to pretend I know exactly what he is saying even though it is only my imagination that is speaking to me.

The truck's horn startles me. Something is happening. I move the camera around and that's when I realize that I am in the wrong business.

X. YOUR CHALICE FORGETS

He says, "We're all in danger, you know."

"I'm aware."

"What are you doing about it?"

"I don't know. You?"

"Waiting."

"For what?"

"For what?" he says. "What do you think? The full moon? The black sun? The cows to come home? The fat lady to sing? What do *you* think I'm waiting for?"

"I don't know. I really don't."

"Well, I'll let you figure that out. Until then…"

"But you said we're in danger."

"Yes."

"It doesn't bother you?"

"I didn't say that."

"You didn't say much of anything."

"I answered your question, didn't I?"

"Not really. I don't even think it was my question."

"You asked if I know we're in danger. I said yes."

"So now what?"

"I told you. I'm waiting."

"I'm terrified."

"You should be."

"What?"

"I said you should be," he says. "Our situation is terrifying."

"Thanks."

"It's the truth."

"I know."

"You're welcome."

"I was being sarcastic."

"Me, too."

XI. MATHEMATICAL THOUGHTS OF G-D

With nothing but a whisper, the manikins silence the heavens. They carve towers from obsidian. They whisper omens and create doors to something akin to infinity. They do their business there. They whisper our names and grant us entry.

Hold close your videotapes, your magnetic idolatry, your photographic evidence, your gold and silver apparitions, your tenebrous documents. Hold closer still your maps of Kokebet and Nogah, your recordings of brittle stars and their songs, your paper-thin masques, your book of conspiratorial codes.

We must have a record of every transaction. We must have a record of each and every one of our businesses no matter how small, how insignificant in the scope of the universe and its cities. The format of the data is not as important as the data itself, of course. We shall store everything in any way we can and hope to hear the whispering that will open doors to multiple opportunities, new jobs, new business.

Let us make a circle around the towers and send our data to G-d. Let us make a square and build walls to keep in the heat of information which is our last powerful weapon. Let us do our business in the public arena for our acts of business are acts of love.

You can play your videotapes. You can read your hefty tomes. But before you attempt to whisper back to the manikins, you must get your papers in order. Whether we end up being destroyed or not is inconsequential. We will always relive our fate.

Both Gog and Magog will fall. They will collapse in silent ruin. They will blanket the universe in grey tones. They will provide us with insecurity and paperwork.

They will arouse our grey matter. They will create holes that can never truly be filled. They will stimulate our private machines of electro-shock therapy and psychotherapeutic magnetism. They will rekindle our passion for fresh air and solid ground and pure white stars and cloudless moonlight. They will help us relive the moment of our creation.

They will, they will, they will. Show us.

We are always in danger.

Amen.

SODOMY IN NINE-ELEVEN LAND

FIGURE 1. The buildings are endless.

I. SUDDENLY SWEEPING LEGS

We were told to sit tight.

I didn't know what that meant.

We were sitting quietly, patiently…when it happened. You couldn't expect us to be any more calm. But when it happened we were suddenly criminals on the verge of mental collapse. We needed to sit tight and it would all be taken care of, would all be over soon. I didn't understand that logic, if it was any logic at all. I really didn't know. Logic is a bizarre thing in that type of situation.

I decided to lose consciousness and refuse to regain it. Would that work? I did not know if that would work at all but anything was worth a try. Anything was better than sitting tight and being calm all the time, all through the frantic timeline of tragedy and our attempting to be composed under fire.

Despite my calm exterior, I was actually quite worried. That shouldn't be a surprise, though, considering what I was going through, considering what everyone was going through. I am not an island. No man is. I am affected by everything, anything, all things, at all times. I was not in isolation. I was never in isolation. I am not in isolation.

My interior was a wreck, a car crash, a plane crash, a family tragedy, financial misfortune. My body was sitting tight but my soul was not.

II. TAKE AWAY

When he regains consciousness, Billy opens his eyes and coughs up gritty, dusty phlegm. He is lying on his back so he slowly sits up, cringing in pain and looks down at his body which is covered in dust and translucent slime.

He remembers nothing except his name.

Billy.

He is sitting on the hard asphalt of an alleyway. Car horns and roaring engines echo down the alley, supplying him with the ambient sounds of city life. Billy stands up, looks around, and sees he is standing in the shadow of a huge tower. While staring up at it, he walks down the alley and out onto the sidewalk. He notices there isn't just one huge tower above him but two. They are shiny and majestic, like two giant shimmering idols reaching up into the sky, reaching up high as if to show its superiority over the surrounding buildings.

Billy is in awe. They are beautiful but imposing like two parents standing over their young children. A curt grunt of a passerby breaks Billy's concentration.

"Move it," a man in a suit says, holding a cell phone up to his ear.

Billy says, "Sorry," and then steps aside only to be bumped into by a chunky woman in a purple business suit. Holding a cell phone up to her ear, she gives him a look of disgust and walks away.

Cars and buses flood the streets, spitting exhaust and noise into the air. Billy looks around and dodges a few more pedestrians. A teenager jostles him, cursing while punching buttons on his cell phone. An old man with a baseball cap almost knocks Billy down to the ground. The man says, "Watch where you're going."

Billy looks at the man's shirt that displays two machine guns over a red, white, and blue background. Big black words say: *All Gave Some – Some Gave All*. He decides not to answer the man but instead moves up against the side of a restaurant, not wanting to get in the wall of anyone else. Again he looks up at the towers.

His awe quickly turns to terror.

III. BAD THEATRE

Everything is a target. Even here in my small town of just over ten thousand people, even here.

Driving on these roads is unsafe. There are buses that could collide with you. There are erratic drivers and drunk drivers and elderly drivers who should not be driving at all. Before you know it, you could be crushed between two automobiles. No one deserves that sort of fate, being sent off to some metallic hell.

I don't take buses. I cannot be at the mercy of another's driving. I don't trust anyone in that manner. The bus drivers are overworked and underpaid. They have not slept enough. They may have a hangover. They may be under the influence of drugs both legal and illicit. I won't take that risk.

There are too many accidents. There are too many unknown factors that can result in my passing away. No one wants to pass away and most people fear it but I probably fear it the most. I fear no shame in admitting my anxiety. I do not disguise my worry in metaphors and myths. I am petrified at the thought of dying. I am even more terrified at the prospect of dying in some sort of spectacle. I do not want my death to be the center of attention. I do not want an audience to my annihilation. I do not want to experience that existential rape. I do not want my death to be recorded in any way or any form. I do not want anyone to have the ability to witness my death over and over again as if some sort of morbid, psychodramatic ritual.

When I was a child I had a dream that a space shuttle crashed in my backyard. I can still remember standing in its shadow, standing in utter terror at the metallic monolith that could have crushed me at any moment.

Everything is a target. Everything is a disease that spreads and destroys both itself and everything around it. I'm being melodramatic. I'm being truthful. I'm being a worrywart. I'm being illogical. I'm being honest. I'm a walking target for death and destruction, for disease and the judgment of some angry hypothetical god.

IV. DRAMANAUT

Billy hears a rumbling from the base of one of the towers.

Then: an explosion. Fiery debris bursts out into the air and gray-brown dust falls to the ground. People on the streets scream and shriek in horror and shock. They spit expletives into the air. Hands cover mouths and eyes.

Billy looks back up at the dual towers and sees that one of them is on fire, one of the higher stories smoking and spitting flames along with office supplies, metal shards, and fatalistic jumpers.

An explosion hits the other tower. More debris and screaming. Papers, staplers, desks, and unidentifiable office junk litter the ground along with body parts and flaming pieces of jetsam. Billy stares at the towers in awe. It is a beautiful sight not because he relishes the destruction of the towers but because the sight is so overpowering and fear-inspiring that he can't help but feel as if he is in the presence of something as majestic as a deity.

The dual towers smoke and flames lick out of the higher floors like tongues.

The first tower falls. It collapses like a stack of dusty blocks. A bulbous cloud of ash speeds from the base of the building down the city streets enveloping the crowds of frightened onlookers. Billy runs into the alleyway and down a stairwell. He huddles in fear. Even though he can't see the ash, he can smell and taste it.

The dirty cloud enters the alleyway and Billy is left to huddle in a blanket of black-grey grit. He loses consciousness while hearing people on the street babble about airplanes and pagans.

V. WE ARE HELD TO IMPOSSIBLE STANDARDS

"How long since you've left the house?"

"I left the house today. To come here."

"I mean other than that and other than to go to work. When was the last time you left the house for something other than that?"

"I don't know."

"Approximately."

"Two weeks, maybe. Two and a half."

"How do you feel about that?"

"What do you mean?"

"By staying inside most of the time, have you felt a greater sense of safety and security?"

"No, not really."

"Then what is the isolation doing for you? Mentally, I mean."

"It's keeping me safe."

"Physically safe?"

"Yeah."

"That's not the only type of well-being we, as people, have to worry about. Your mental stability is just as important…if not more so. If a person is not mentally healthy, they are often not physically healthy."

"I'm not talking about health. I'm talking about staying alive."

"And so what is it that you are afraid of if you were to go out and maybe go to the store or take a walk around the neighborhood?"

"Lots of things."

"Such as?"

"Getting into a car accident. Getting hit by a car. Being killed by someone."

"Do you find these to be valid concerns?"

"Yeah."

"What about your drive to work? Do you feel somewhat protected from those dangers when you drive to work?"

"No, but it's something I have to do."

"So you're aware of a certain sense of responsibility as an adult. You know you have to go to work in order to support yourself and that motivates you to forget about the dangers you feel are present."

"I don't forget about them."

"But you don't let them prevent you from driving to work. See what I'm saying? Your sense of responsibility is quite strong. That's a good thing."

"I guess."

"You need to realize that in order to have a healthy mind, you need to go out and enjoy yourself outside of the house, outside of work. You'll find the dangers will diminish. They'll no longer pose such an overpowering threat to your well-being."

"Maybe."

"It's not a maybe. You can do it. You are not so far along that you can't regain that confidence in life, in your ability to succeed when you feel threatened by dangers that may or may not be realistic."

"The things I'm afraid of aren't unrealistic. People get into car accidents every day. People get killed all the time. I just don't want to play those odds."

"But things happen in the home, too. People die of accidents or of illness and disease. What's stopping something from happening in your home? Or at work?"

"I've thought about that, too. I've thought about diseases. I'm starting to be terrified of viruses. I've been thinking about biological terrorism lately."

"Now, why would you do something like that?"

"I saw something on T.V. about it and then I just started reading a bunch of books about it."

"You know that's not healthy, that morbid fascination."

"I don't think it's morbid. I just want to be aware."

"Awareness of every danger is not going to offer protection to them."

"It might help."

"Are you sure about that?"

"Yeah. I've thought about this a lot."

"I know you have and I think that's a big part of the problem. You think too much about the negative consequences of living, or rather the *possible* consequences, without thinking about the positives, about the things you can gain from going out there and actually living."

"Maybe so but I don't see any way around it. I can't turn my awareness off. I can't forget the things I know."

"But you can train your mind not to focus on them."

"I don't know about that."

"I do. I think you can do it. I'm sure of it, actually."

"If you say so."

"I do say so. You need to let me help you, though."

"Well, that's why I'm here. I'm looking for help."

VI. AUTUMNAL OCCULT

When Billy awakes, he still doesn't remember anything about himself except for his name and the cloudy memory of the previous day's events. For a few seconds he thinks that the destruction of the dual towers is just a dream. Once he realizes that he can't open his eyes due to crusty ash, he knows that it has been real. He spits on his hand and washes his face. He coughs up gritty, dusty phlegm.

The alley is covered with a foot of dust and metallic debris. Slivers of glass twinkle in the gloom, burning Billy's already sore eyes. Instead of the funeral silence or screaming horror that he expects, Billy hears the sounds of construction. He gets up and walks to the edge of the alley and looks out into the street. All over people are cleaning up the streets. The rubble that has been the dual towers is now being used to rebuild them both. Hundreds of citizens are on scaffolds helping to reconstruct the towers while still coughing up blood and wiping dust out of their eyes. Many of them cry out in righteous anger while operating their power tools.

Billy can't believe it. The people building do not look like professional builders. They look like housewives, officer workers, bus drivers, children, teenagers in trendy clothing, and practically every other type of person he can imagine.

They work like hyperactive ants. For hours Billy stands in the middle of the sidewalk and watches them. Occasionally someone yells over at him saying something like "Why aren't you helping?" Billy just shrugs and stutters incoherently. He doesn't think there is a right answer to that question.

By the end of the day, both towers are fully rebuilt but now each is a story higher than it had been the previous day. The citizen-builders had rebelled against the destruction itself by extending the towers pass their previous height.

There is a roaring sound, a rumble underground, and then an explosion in one of the towers. Billy can't believe that it is all happening again. Just like clockwork, the second tower bursts into flames, too. Soon they both fall, causing monstrous clouds of dust to speed through the streets, again enveloping the crowds that gathered in the streets. People holding their cell phones or coffee cups are swept up and are blown around like leaves.

Billy runs into the alley, hoping to find shelter from the concrete-metal-debris storm that is chasing him. Again he loses consciousness against a brick wall, another blanket of dust covering him like a dirty quilt.

VII. IF JANUS IS CAPTURED

Maybe if I sit here and close my eyes. Maybe if I sit here, close my eyes, and watch the past erupt into nonexistence, my own nonexistence, my own frail conception of the past, my own unstable recollection of the events, of the whole world blacking out in just a few hours, all as a result of manmade machines making mankind brutal in finite ways without verification of the infinite.

No men will ever awake to virgins smoking hashish. No men will swim in celestial pools of water that resonate with the universe. No men will find wings sprouting from their backs as they devour the fruit of some paradise tree.

Maybe I'll sit here and fantasize about another timeline, another historical event, another monumental moment in our lives, something that's akin to a celebration and not a mass funeral. I don't care for viewpoints or opinions. I just want everything to be whole again. I want all things to be new again. I want a sex drive again. I want there to be buildings everywhere. I want there to be criminals being hanged in the street. I want there to be helping hands wherever I turn. I want there to be kind words and honest appraisals of our ineptitude. I want there to be the purest feelings ever felt in the streets of our departure and our arrival.

I talk to myself and I don't make any sense of it. All my words seem rehearsed. Have I gone through this before? Have I rehearsed this in a dream? Have I failed to remember the process, the procedure? Will I survive? Do I deserve to survive?

My reactions are normal, I suppose, but that just means I'm as common as the next person. Do I deserve to expect more from myself? If I expect more, will I get more? Will I get what I deserve? What do I deserve? Do I deserve the same as the others?

The process is a complex one. We all function like simple machines in an old barn primed for collapse. We are lost in the haze of psychological disruption, psychic masochism as victims, as play actors in a primitive Grand Guignol performance, all stone weapons and teeth, flea-infested hair and disease. We are all in the high risk category. We are looking for cancer but find only unknown entities spreading in sparkling displays like fireworks, screaming ulcers.

Maybe I'll close my eyes and accept what I deserve. I probably don't deserve to survive but if I do, then I'll send a letter to the president and give him the bad news.

VIII. KIA SURVIVAL ZOS

Billy wakes up at dawn and sneaks through the rubble and sees more people gathering at the base of where the towers had stood as they got ready to build them up again. He walks around, hoping to be inconspicuous.

He sees a group of men in camouflaged business suits setting up explosives at the base of the towers. One of the men, a short man with slicked back blond hair, is talking to another, pointing up into the sky and gesturing. The man he is talking to is tall and stocky. He is holding a bundle of explosives under his left arm. Billy knows this because the box says "EXPLOSIVES".

Billy wonders why no one else finds their presence strange. He is terrified and confused.

So he runs back into the alley.

Instinctively he knows that no one would believe him. Billy cuddles up next to a cardboard box in a fetal position and waits for the construction and subsequent explosive attacks against the towers.

He falls asleep and dreams of guns, prisons, and a woman who is waving a flag while soldiers start to shoot their load of red, white, and blue sperm into her bowels that splatter her insides like machine-gun fire.

IX. EMERGING EPIDEMICS

I'm not freaking out. Okay, I'm not. I'm not freaking out, I'm not making a scene, I'm not getting out of control. I'm keeping my composure. I'm calm.

What this boils down to is this: what I'm hoping for is some sort of smooth resolution to this entire thing. Is that to much to ask? I'm filled with anxiety. I'm filled with dread. I'm filled with that childhood feeling of being left behind by my parents. Who is going to look after me? Who is going to assure that I have a future?

I'm not going into the city. There are no buses, no trains, no cars, nothing that will be able to bring me or my anxious nervous system into the labyrinthine junkyard. If I venture out into the city, all I'll see is graffiti: sigils initiating the new software in the Swiss cheese of my corrupted brain. I'll begin to see wonders and construct false structures for posterity, for scrapbooks, for the books I'll publish under my father's name.

These things that were destroyed were our precious things and will never again fulfill us.

We might as well pack up our stuff and leave but…

I'm not freaking out.

I'm not losing control.

To lose control is to lose faith and I am not losing my faith, not surrendering to nihilism, to the bleak outlook of the future that many in my position are subscribing to. They sit in their chairs and they write their treatises on our pain and devastation, deconstruction, some postmodern metafictional pap that doesn't ring true in any country, in any century, in any real human mind. No human mind needs alternatives to real tragedy or real faith or both of them combined in a fireball of reciprocity.

I'm not freaking out, though, or at least I'm doing my best not to.

X. PETE AND REPEAT GET ON A PLANE

The next day there is another attack and another reconstruction. The towers are even taller than they were before.

Billy hears a voice in the street cry out, "Why aren't you helping?" Billy walks out to the edge of the alley and sees a woman standing in the street, looking at the towers just as he had done the day before. She is wearing a scarf and nothing else. Her moon-shaped ass is a pale lighthouse in the dusty air of the street. There is a woman in a jogging suit right next to her, asking the naked woman why she wasn't assisting in the reconstruction.

Billy feels his penis swell.

He says, "Hey."

The scarf woman turns around but says nothing.

Again Billy says, "Hey." He motions to her to come to the alley. She slowly turns away from the woman in the jogging suit and walks towards Billy, her eyes are blue and piercing.

Billy looks down from her eyes to her dark, bushy pubic hair. He stares at it until she is standing right in front of him.

She says, "Yeah?"

He grabs her arm and brings her into the alley, not sure why he is doing it but suspecting that it is an instinct to protect her from both the oncoming destruction of the towers, the harassment of the people on the street, and the suspicious men in camouflaged suits.

Billy grabs her just in time. There is more rumbling and another explosion. Screams of horror, shock, and vows of revenge. But through that noise, Billy hears the naked woman say, "Look."

Another explosion.

The men in camouflaged suits point at the exploding towers, appreciating their handiwork. Are they doing what he thinks they are doing? Are they responsible for the explosions? No, no, they can't be. That would be absurd...and unethical.

XI. CLOP

It's not that I want to take so many pills. I don't want to be dependant on chemicals to relieve my anxiety, to be able to venture into the city, into the arms of a possible future that will destroy me.

I see symbols everywhere. I see numbers as clues, clues to my arrival at a goal I do not want to meet. I see smoke and flames. I see sunken faces and ash. I see all these things on the T.V. and in magazines. I see flyers on telephone poles. I see phone numbers that bloom into dangerous meetings.

I will take no more pills.

XII. AN HONOR

They are symbols of growth and destruction, rebirth and even more destruction.

The towers have been rebuilt so high that Billy can't even see the tops of them. The outsides of the building are covered with people still working on the construction. Furiously they work to make the towers more magnificent and awe-inspiring than before.

He sees the men in camouflaged suits. Billy knows what they have in mind. They are going to blow the buildings up again yet no one even gives them a second glance because they look official. They look like men from a government agency. For some reason Billy knows that this is the case. They are probably just following orders from the top: destroy the buildings and let the citizens come together to rebuild while their national pride surges to new heights.

Billy wants to stop them himself but knows that he is too terrified to do so. Instead, he points at the men and shouts gibberish in hopes of other people noticing the men. He hopes they notice that these men are not just investigators or law enforcement but rather saboteurs who are planning for more monumental destruction followed by patriotic reconstruction by the zealous masses. It is a cycle of concrete-metal-glass murder and rebirth.

No one notices.

XIII. WHO IS LEFT

You can stay here for as long as you need to. I know things are really messed up out there and people shouldn't be alone at a time like this. I'm sensitive to these things, you know. I'm not inhuman.

I recorded six hours of it onto VHS tape but I think something happened and it didn't record correctly. That's a shame because it would have been a nice memento.

Do you want to reenact the events?

Do you want to fantasize about being a hero?

Do you want to fantasize about being a victim?

Do you want to write your own narrative?

I think everyone, everywhere, at all times should be thinking about these things, about the parallel universes that contain this event in an infinite number of ways and we can all become dizzy with the possibilities and maybe we can find one, just one place and time where the events transpired in ways that weren't so devastating. We can hope.

No one is left but us and that's okay because you and I will light candles and tell stories and write words on walls so we can remember everything and everyone at all times.

We'll ignore the danger because otherwise we'll collapse under psychological torment and the overwhelming fear that our lives are nothing but blips on a malfunctioning radar.

So that's that.

XIV. NO SIR

Billy is really William T. Roanoke of Tom's River, New Jersey.

He has always hated being called Billy. He prefers William. But such is life. People do what's easiest for themselves.

William inhales the ash, the smoke, the tiny pieces of fiery paper, the asbestos, the cement dust, liquefied plastic, the jet fuel fumes. Everything goes in, nothing comes out. William falls to his knees and reads the side of a taxi. He thinks about how expensive the rates are.

He vomits into a pile of white powder. He thinks about scooping the powder up, putting it into a batch of envelopes, and sending them away to random people. The randomness itself will be a tribute to the loop of destruction he is witnessing.

There is no end to the reconstruction.

William T. Roanoke relieves himself of his identity and decides to let himself be nothing but the shape of things to come, all the possible lives of each victim, each damaged shell.

There is no end to the destruction.

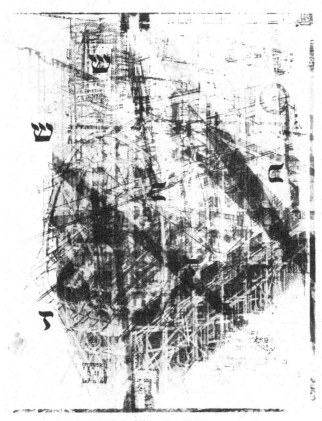
FIGURE 2. The buildings are lost.

IMPORTANT!

In 1956, Dr. Thomas Griffith diagnosed a patient with a viral infection. This infection had caused the patient to display a wide variety of symptoms including fever, jaundice, confusion, auditory hallucinations, diarrhea, and heart palpitations.

After additional testing, Dr. Griffith concluded that the viral infection was a result of a more serious malady. The patient (we will refer to him as BARRY) had previously shown signs of mental illness and in Dr. Griffith's opinion, this mental illness caused the spread of a virus that ended up infecting multiple parts of BARRY's body.

BARRY, however, insisted that the cause of his condition was his working at the crash site of an airplane. He stated that his had inhaled noxious fumes while cleaning up pieces of the fuselage. Dr. Griffith dismissed this because the symptoms BARRY had displayed did not match those of any sort of respiratory illness. In fact, BARRY's lungs appeared quite healthy.

After even more extensive tests, Dr. Griffith recommended that BARRY see another physician, Dr. Joshua Drake, located in Manhattan. The patient refused, stating that he never travels into the city for fear that the buildings would collapse around him. Dr. Griffith then recommended he seek psychiatric help to which BARRY replied, "Those types of structures don't work on me, doc."

See Figure 3.

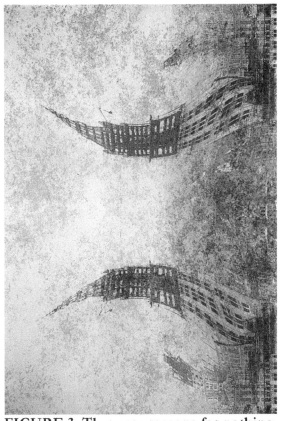

FIGURE 3. There are reasons for nothing.

A NOTE

Tatiana Drake was one of the lesser known starlets who were featured in Ian Woolworth's "pretty girl" films of the 1940s and 1950s. She was only 17 years old when she co-starred in *All the Girls in the City* in 1942 and also appeared in Woolworth's last film *City's Last Light* in 1959. After that, she disappeared from the Hollywood scene and was rumored to have started directing low budget documentary films under the pseudonym Antonio Corbelli. **See Figure 4.**

FIGURE 4. Finally, the cell collapses.

To put it plainly, I simply do not want my wife bringing my son into the city. Buses are unsafe. Subways are unsafe. Taxi cabs are unsafe. The streets are, of course, unsafe. Once someone is in the city, they are at the mercy of a cluster of tall monoliths that symbolize nothing but man's loosening grip on reality. They symbolize the insane death throes of a desperate species. I do not want my wife to bring my son into the city. There is no way to protect him. There is no way to protect *anyone*. **See Figure 5.**

FIGURE 5. We are subways unrelated to planes.

ANTICITY COMMITTEE OF EASTERN SAYREVILLE

Resource 23.a.44.
October 22, 2001

(a.) multiple myeloma
(b.) air quality
(c.) Corps of Engineers
(d.) respirators
(e.) latex
(f.) 55 cancers

…a sexual assault committed post-disaster, according to sources.

First responders targeted for discrete hypnagogic assassination.

> Susan Bayley
> John Lagotto
> Frank Mahoney
> Felicia Williamson

(g.) post-mortem sabotage
(h.) janitorial district
(i.) Stuyvesant protests
(j.) form constant jet fuel
(k.) official hypnic jerk

He spent six months at the site.

THE AIR QUALITY IS SAFE AND ACCEPTABLE

Chemical sensitivity. Are you positive?

ISS image taken the day of the event. We should monitor everything at all times. Something similar to what was found in Lyme.

...because of the additional assaults...

...further studies would indicate a link between exposures and...SEE FIGURE 6.

FIGURE 6. No one bothers to jump.

William watches the atrocity and is sickened by it.

The reconstruction has no effect on him. The damage had been done. The dust is still in the air. The blood is still on the ground. It has leaked into the sewers and into the soil of gardens, penetrating the roots of plants and flowers. The air is scarred with vibrations and chemtrails. Nothing will ever be the same, even after the rebuilding of the idols.

William is afraid to move. He is afraid to think. He is afraid to predict. He is afraid to plan things. He is afraid to remember things. He is afraid to create new memories.

He decides he is done. He's done.

He sits tight and waits.

He just waits.

FIGURE 7. We are our own best friends.

Found Objectives

soviet

new post in the city

XXX

recovered at the scene

five points ov haShem

bodydomelights

INVOCATION OF A
BLAST EVENT

"What our children have to fear is not the cars on the highways of tomorrow but our own pleasure in calculating the most elegant parameters of their deaths."
-J.G. Ballard

The act of allowing the dust to rise and the clouds to fall…

The chance has arrived and I speak through the sirens and hope to be heard. My voice cut the officer. I was not allowed to resist. But Charles Bishop allowed me to read his note before he crashed.

You have sympathy, I said to him. You have a lot of sympathy but you neglect to see the forest for the trees (or the city for the buildings).

There doesn't need to be problems. We confide in strangers and cause them serious health problems. I am able to manage stress very well. I can manage. I can manage.

Can you cope, Charles? Can you cope?

What if you miss your flight?

That's not possible. That's impossible.

I'm unable to miss it…

We are gathered here today…

The marriage of heaven and earth: boom!
The marriage of brick and mortar: boom!
The marriage of fear and faith: boom!

I'd like to know the route you take to work. Can you draw me a map? Can you give me directions? Can you, can you, can you?

Okay, so here's the plan. (here's the plane)

We are getting out of here on the 23rd. Don't ask me how…just trust me.

Don't use that skin cream. You know damn well it's making you depressed. You are acting…not like yourself. What will your parents say?

There is no time like the present.

Plans for vacation.

Ha!

Now we shall see if the doctors were right.

Terribly, terribly ashamed…

He was a good boy. I'll tell you that much. I'll tell anyone who will listen. He was a good boy. There is no way he did this on his own. Someone must have put him up to it or made him do it or he didn't do it at all. I don't care what they say.

The materials? I don't know how he… I have no idea where he could have gotten that stuff and I don't believe that he got it himself. Like I said, I think someone else made him do it or put the blame on him. There's no way, just no way he could have… I mean, if you knew him like we did you would know he is not capable of doing something like that.

He loved animals. He loved baseball. He loved fishing. He was a normal kid, a wonderful bright young man. You people don't know him.

Don't know him.

"I'm assuming you know why you're here?"

"No, I do not."

"It's about your performance."

"My performance?"

"Yes."

"What about it?"

"We've been dissatisfied with it."

"In what way?"

"In every way. Your performance is poor. I don't know how else to say it. You seem…unqualified for your position. I'm not even sure how you managed to stay here this long."

"This is ridiculous."

"I'm sure you feel that way but…it's the truth."

"I'd like to see my union rep."

"You can do what you like but I'm fairly sure they will see things the same way."

"Bullshit."

"You can leave now."

Something doesn't sound right…

We drove through the industrial park, looking for the doctor, looking for any sign that we'd have a great Friday night. I told Frank that he should probably not…indulge in the festivities. He always has a bad reaction. He gets crazy. He takes off his clothes. He breaks windows. He hurts himself. But still…he insisted on coming along, on finding the doctor, on finding something to take away the pain.

Frank lost his daughter a year ago and hasn't been the same since.

I can't blame him for doing what he does. I can't imagine what I would do if I was in his position. His daughter was his whole life. It devastated him. I'm shocked he didn't kill himself, actually. I know that's a terrible thing to say but it's true. I was really worried he'd overdose on purpose or jump off the bridge behind his house. But no…he kept on living.

He quit his job at Litton Industries and went to work doing security for one of the buildings in the industrial park.

That's where he met the doctor.

I figured I didn't deserve the disease so obviously there was no fairness in the world. I've believed in God for most of my life but once I got sick it was like…well, it was like the rug got pulled out from under me and I realized that nothing is out there or at least nothing I thought there was. Why the hell would God let a person get this disease? I didn't deserve it. I was a good person.

That's changed, though, and I'm not afraid to admit it. I'm not a nice person. I've made a decision to be the worst I can be and that includes spreading the disease to others. Do they deserve it? No but life isn't fair. It wasn't fair for me so it shouldn't be fair for anyone else.

I smear my semen on doorknobs. I leave trails of blood everywhere. I would like to infect everyone who has the misfortune to be alive.

This is how my world ends…and so it shall be for everyone else.

I'm a human bomb.

I will finish my work with an explosion.

I will corrupt society with my gore.

God help you.

There is no such thing as peace…

You had no business being in Madrid.

You knew it was a mistake yet you still went.

You should have known better.

You should have taken your mother's advice and just stayed home.

She knows you better than anyone else.

Yet you still went to Madrid.

Yet you still met with the man who claims he is your father.

What did he teach you?

What wisdom, what skills did he pass on to you?

You should call your mother back.

You should tell her you were wrong.

You should tell her that you had no idea that it was going to happen that way.

She may not believe you but you should still tell her.

You should call your mother.

Richard lights a match under the photograph and lets it burn to ashes. He runs the sink. The evidence is now gone. His fingernails are black. His brain is parasite-ridden. He sits down on the kitchen floor. He masturbates out of desperation and guilt.

He is incapable of reaching climax.

The telephone rings.

He makes no attempt to answer it.

There is no one he'd like to talk to. In fact, he is sure whoever is calling has bad news for him.

He stands up. He walks into the garage. He gets his rifle. He goes outside. He waits.

He waits.

Depraved Lowland Majesty…

"It's set?"

"It's set."

"Ten minutes, correct?"

"Yeah, ten minutes."

"Three on the perimeter?"

"Yeah."

"Five inside?"

"Yeah."

"This is going to be spectacular."

"It will."

"You ready?"

"I'm ready."

"God bless."

"God bless."

Christian digs through the rubble. He pockets several souvenirs: a watch, a necklace, several teeth. He takes photographs of the scene. He will upload them to the internet tonight. He will send them to the women he is trying to seduce.

A police officer walks around the corner, sees Christian, and shines a flashlight.

The officer shouts.

Christian slowly stands up, arms raised, smiling with crooked teeth and staring with crooked eyes.

"Sorry…," he says to the officer. He runs.

The police officer chases him, catches up, brings out his taser, shoots Christian.

Christian falls to the ground, convulsing, and then disappears into fiery ash.

No End of the World...

Consonants poke candent holes through my doctrine. If there are vowels, they are hiding under the shroud of a guttural dogma encrypted within an interoffice memo. The moth-reptile starts to defecate on me....greenish liquid splattering the prophet's eyes. I embrace all of it and shudder into a trance. Nonsense words leak out of my mouth like vomit.

And the theater there is made of drugged diamond planes...a person submits to and becomes a possession of...and that's that, the last showing of that Middle Eastern film. Behind the theater there is a field and children build forts and make a mess of it but that's okay because no one pays any mind. They're just kids. The boy stands in front of his class and reads from his notebook, "At the core of the city, the fungal magnificence of the building enthralls all who circle it..."

Pompeii, second generation, still exists. The dust-mummies running through the streets. They exist. I can feel the heat and taste the grit but it is just my brain working overtime to communicate to me the hallucinations implanted in me. Everything I see and hear, smell, everything, is a result of the pedophile doctors and scientists who have installed memory clusters in my brain and long-term suppositories that buzz and dissolve. I see cobra heads and minarets and bearded men spinning. My eleven year old brain not knowing what or who or where, it had shut off and I had slept for 3 days.

You are my mother. You are not the gatekeeper of knowledge. Yes, you married him but I am a part of him or rather, he is a part of me. Therefore, if any force is to destroy his body, I am to know about it. I am to be privy to any knowledge no matter how destructive it may be to my psyche. Not since childhood have you been responsible for that part of my existence.

The wallpaper is ancient: pictures of cartoon patients smiling while cartoon doctors examine them with old-fashioned instruments. I sit on the examining table and get a closer look at the yellowing pictures: water bottles, tin toys, plastic toys, wooden toys, papers with scribbles, pictures drawn by young children for mom/dad (no real talent evident but all the love in the world), condom wrappers, syringes, computer corpses, tubes of glue, magazines with gossip in heat, covered in sweat and jet fuel.

It makes sense being that sexual dysfunction was one of the side effects. But even with that in mind, my blaming of the medication didn't eliminate the stress. A part of me thinks I am somehow broken. It is a paranoid midlife crisis even though I am only thirty-one years old.

Inside the basement, three men finish work copying several texts. One of them remarks how much the words look like "scribble-scrabble" and that makes him laugh. Though the cement room makes for an unconventional scriptorium, it is the only place the men could expect to complete their work without fear of interruption or infiltration. It is a psychic safe house, a bastion of textual security. It breathes when they breathe. It burps when they burp.

"So our government is sending out death squads?"

"Because of this possibility, I do not even entertain the idea of joining in their conversation to prove them wrong, to bring their ignorance to the forefront of their consciousnesses. I am a gentleman, really."

"Light."

"What?"

"The light."

"So what?"

"Blinded me."

"So what?"

"You knew I was going to come calling eventually. Let's not pretend we do favors for nothing. It's give and take."

"Yeah, I know."

"So, I'm officially cashing this one in."

"Christ, Roy." Automobiles explode. No one read the roadside announcements. There is no parking here. There is no parking anywhere. The situation is too dangerous. Just yesterday a judge's car was blown into fiery bits, killing a handful of innocent people who had the misfortune of wanting an autograph or an appeal.

A victim is a victim is a victim and a hole is a hole is a hole. That's what I've learned and that's what I'm saying to you all now. When I say "you all" I really just mean you because, let's face it, only one person is going to be reading this at a time. I don't imagine my little scribble-scrabble is going to make it into some sort of book club or be read aloud at a funeral or something. I walk out of the bathroom and seem them scattered on the floor and crudely taped to the walls. The pictures are all the same: a grainy black-and-white reproduction of an architectural blueprint.

Second, even if it did happen like that (and as I stated above, it most certainly did not) I would have been justified in my actions because when we come down to it, a person needs to accept his or her position in society and act accordingly. Not everyone can do what their neighbor can nor should they be expected to try just for the appeasement of the rest of society. That's not to say I'll give up. No. I am many things but I'm not a pessimist or fatalist. Pessimism is for lazy, bitter people who lack the self-confidence to attempt to change their lives.

I am the only journalist who is willing to sit down with the MAN, across from the MAN, and ask the questions, tackle the topics, dare to delve into things no one has had the courage to do before. I will stare the MAN in the face and seek the TRUTH. The MAN is normal looking. He is nondescript. He is quite boring.

But he is also impotent.

I am no fool. I know my place in the scheme of things even if that place is somewhere tucked away between the pages of a moldy apocalyptic book in some unkempt library of a suburban town that is both small and insignificant, a town that has ceased to grow in population as a result of the outdated information in their town hall meetings as well as the library where the moldy apocalyptic manuscript is located, harboring divine and not-so-divine symbology misshapen by archaic phraseology and whatever else you'd expect from such an ancient tome in an unimportant town.

You are in an industrial park. You are standing on the asphalt of a parking lot of a corporation named MONS GRAUPIUS, INC. You wonder what they make but the sign is too abstract and gives no indication as to the business they are in.

"Christ, Roy."

But what now? Both my parents are gone and their house, like all their possessions inside, is just a decomposing reminder of their finite importance in the scheme of things. Automobiles, mailboxes, and storefronts explode. The situation is dangerous. Just yesterday a police officer's car was blown into bits, killing several young people who had the misfortune of being stopped for driving while under the influence of hallucinogens.

The din translates into mantras that sprout digitalized incarnations of their hard work, the sweat of their brows, their underarms, and their grey matter. Someone is behind me now. It's the new guy but fortunately he doesn't say a word to me. He is staring out the window. Everyone is staring out the window. The structures are just shapes against the sky. They do not represent anything except shapes. Their significance does not extend beyond being simple structures in the midst of other structures. Sometimes I fall asleep to the sound of ominous spheres rolling down the hallway outside my door. Sometimes I awake to the sound of spherical doom opening and closing doors in the hallway outside. Sometimes I sit and listen to the soft babbling of my empty room as it smears interrupted silence on the surface of my gloom.

Every decision is difficult.

But everything is more difficult for me.

Don't be so melodramatic. You're a grown man. Shit or get off the pot. Do what you want to do or don't do anything at all. Do whatever you want, when you want.

So what now?

He says, "We're all in danger, you know."

"Everything's fine," I say to him.

Something is quite wrong.

It goes without saying that I should probably explain the events leading up to my current situation. This situation I'm in is dire, yes, but I've pretty much accepted my fate or accepted it as much as you'd expect any person to under the circumstances. You lurk on the threshold. Then there is an explosion.

Someone once told me my body was primed for death.

Like always, I had responded with skepticism.

You ask if anyone is in the room.

No one answers you.

You ask again.

The two groups are readying along the perimeter. They are disguised, as is to be expected, and they are overloaded with gear they may not even need.

I zoom out.

With nothing but a whisper, the manikins silence the heavens. They carve towers from obsidian. They whisper omens and create doors to something akin to infinity. They do their business there. They whisper our names and grant us entry.

Clean Plots…

I don't have a lot of options.

I have a choice of maybe three things I can do and they are all within the realm of "acts of terror" and whatever other title the kings have given to all orgasmic forms of revolution.

I receive three checks a month. I survive on that money and the occasional donation from Graupius. I don't require much. My life is simple but still: I don't have a lot of options.

The backpack is heavy.

The shoes are uncomfortable.

The package in my stomach is heavy and I am convinced it will break and destroy my bowels. But whatever happens will happen. I cannot change things. Not at this point. I'm on the path and nearing the end.

The end of what?

Who knows?

I don't.

Does it matter?

I suggest you stay home from work today. Keep your kids home from school. The kingdom will arise in shockwaves and perfect thunder. My mind will accompany the holy asses as they slowly walk through the gate, huffing and puffing, and they will BLOW THE HOUSE DOWN.

We are all in danger. Yes, even me. Even me.

So what now? Watch the grey plumes and ash with skin cells and copier paper, coffee cups, paperclips, staplers and Scotch tape, liquid paper fireworks, fluttering manila folders as death-birds.

Hummingbirds.

AND DANGER.

The story is concluded in

YOUR CITIES, YOUR TOMBS

which is available in paperback from

Copeland Valley Press.

Made in the USA
Las Vegas, NV
16 August 2024